I0764371

The Vizier of the Two-Horned Alexander

"'I LENT LARGE SUMS TO THE NOBLE KNIGHTS.'"

The Vizier of the Two-Horned Alexander

Frank R. Stockton
Edited by Paul Dennis Sporer

Illustrated by
Reginald B. Birch

Karanovo Press

ANZA PUBLISHING, Chester, NY 10918
Karanovo Press is an imprint of Anza Publishing

This work is a new, unabridged edition of *The Vizier of the Two-Horned Alexander*, by Frank R. Stockton, originally published in 1899.

Library of Congress Cataloguing-in-Publication Data
Stockton, Frank Richard, 1834-1902.
The vizier of the two-horned Alexander / Frank R. Stockton ; edited by Paul Dennis Sporer.
p. cm.
Originally published: New York : Century Co., 1899.
ISBN 1-932490-07-8 (alk. paper)
1. Immortalism—Fiction.
I. Sporer, Paul D. II. Title.
PS2927.V595 2005
813'.4--dc22 2005021330

The characters and events in this book are fictitious. Any similarity to real persons, living or dead, is purely coincidental and not intended by the author.

∞ This book is printed on acid-free paper.

ISBN 1-932490-07-8 (hardcover)

Contents

Chapter One

I WAS ON A FRENCH STEAMER bound from Havre to New York, when I had a peculiar experience in the way of a shipwreck. On a dark and foggy night, when we were about three days out, our vessel collided with a derelict—a great, heavy, helpless mass, as dull and colorless as the darkness in which she was enveloped. We struck her almost head on, and her stump of a bowsprit was driven into our port bow with such tremendous violence that a great hole—nobody knew of what dimensions—was made in our vessel.

The collision occurred about two hours before daylight, and the frightened passengers who crowded the upper deck were soon informed by the officers that it would be necessary to take to the boats, for the vessel was rapidly settling by the head. Now, of course, all was hurry and confusion. The captain endeavored to assure his passengers that there were boats enough to carry every soul on board, and that there was time enough for them to embark quietly and in order. But as the French people did not understand him when he spoke in English, and as the Americans did not readily comprehend what he said in French, his exhortations were of little avail. With such of their possessions as they could carry, the people crowded into the boats as soon as they were ready, and sometimes before they were ready; and while there was not exactly a panic on board, each man seemed to be inspired with the idea that his safety, and that of his family, if he had one, depended upon precipitate individual action.

I was a young man, traveling alone, and while I was as anxious as anyone to be saved from the sinking vessel, I was not a coward, and I could not thrust myself into a boat when there were women and children behind me who had not yet been provided with places. There were men who did this, and several times I felt inclined to knock one of the poltroons overboard. The deck was well lighted, the steamer was settling slowly, and there was no excuse for the dastardly proceedings which were going on about me. It was not long, however, before almost all of the passengers were safely embarked, and I was preparing to get into a boat which was nearly filled with the officers and crew, when I was touched on the shoulder, and turning, I saw a gentleman whose acquaintance I had made soon after the steamer had left Havre. His name was Crowder. He was a middle-aged man, a New Yorker, intelligent and of a social disposition, and I had found him a very pleasant companion. To my amazement, I perceived that he was smoking a cigar.

"If I were you," said he, "I would not go in that boat. It is horribly crowded, and the captain and second officer have yet to find places in it."

"That's all the more reason," said I, "why we should hurry. I am not going to push myself ahead of women and children, but I've just as much right to be saved as the captain has, and if there are any vacant places, let us get them as soon as possible."

Crowder now put his hand on my shoulder as if to restrain me. "Safety!" said he. "You needn't trouble yourself about safety. You are just as safe where you are as you could possibly be in one of those boats. If they are not picked up soon,—and they may float about for days, — their sufferings and discomforts will be very great. There is a shameful want of accommodation in the way of boats."

"But, my dear sir," said I, "I can't stop here to talk about that. They are calling for the captain now."

"Oh, he's in no hurry," said my companion. "He's collecting his papers, I suppose, and he knows his vessel will not sink under him while he is doing it. I'm not going in that boat; I haven't the least idea of such a thing. It will be odiously crowded, and I assure you, sir, that if the sea should be rough that boat will be dangerous. Even now she is overloaded."

I looked at the man in amazement. He had spoken earnestly, but he was as calm as if we were standing on a sidewalk, and he endeavoring to dissuade me from boarding an overcrowded street-car. Before I could say anything he spoke again.

"I am going to remain on this ship. She is a hundred times safer than any of those boats. I have had a great deal of experience in regard to vessels and ocean navigation, and it will be a long time before this vessel sinks, if she ever sinks of her own accord. She's just as likely to float as that derelict we ran into. The steam is nearly out of her boilers by this time, and nothing is likely to happen to her. I wish you would stay with me. Here we will be safe, with plenty of room, and plenty to eat and drink. When it is daylight we will hoist a flag of distress, which will be much more likely to be seen than anything that can flutter from those little boats. If you have noticed, sir, the inclination of this deck is not greater now than it was half an hour ago. That proves that our bow has settled down to about as far as it is going; hence, I think it quite likely that the water has entered only a few of the forward compartments."

The man spoke so confidently that his words made quite an

impression upon me. I knew that it very often happens that a wreck floats for a long time, and the boat from which the men were now frantically shouting for the captain would certainly be dangerously crowded.

"Stay with me," said Mr. Crowder, "and I assure you, with as much reason as any man can assure any other man of anything in this world, that you will be perfectly safe. This steamer is not going to sink."

There were rapid footsteps, and I saw the captain and his second officer approaching.

"Step back here," said Mr. Crowder, pulling me by the coat. "Don't let them see us. They may drag us on board that confounded boat. Keep quiet, sir, and let them get off. They think they are the last on board."

Involuntarily I obeyed him, and we stood in the shadow of the great funnel. The captain had reached the rail.

"Is everyone in the boats?" he shouted, in French and in English. "Is everyone in the boats? I am going to leave the vessel." I made a start as if to rush toward him, but Crowder held me by the arm.

"Don't you do it," he whispered very earnestly. "I have the greatest possible desire to save you. Stay where you are, and you will be all right. That overloaded boat may capsize in half an hour."

I could not help it; I believed him. My own judgment seemed suddenly to rise up and ask me why I should leave the solid deck of the steamer for that perilous little boat.

I need say but little more in regard to this shipwreck. When the fog lifted, about ten o'clock in the morning, we could see no signs of any of the boats. A mile or so away lay the dull, black line of the derelict, as if she were some savage beast who had bitten and torn

"'DON'T YOU DO IT.'"

us, and was now sullenly waiting to see us die of the wound. We hoisted a flag, union down, and then we went below to get some breakfast. Mr. Crowder knew all about the ship, and where to find everything. He told me he had made so many voyages that he felt almost as much at home on sea as on land. We made ourselves comfortable all day, and at night we went to our rooms, and I slept fairly well, although there was a very disagreeable slant to my berth. The next day, early in the afternoon, our signal of distress was seen by a tramp steamer on her way to New York, and we were taken off.

We cruised about for many hours in the direction the boats had probably taken, and the next day we picked up two of them in a sorry condition, the occupants having suffered many hardships and privations. We never had news of the captain's boat, but the others were rescued by a sailing-vessel going eastward.

Before we reached New York, Mr. Crowder had made me promise that I would spend a few days with him at his home in that city. His family was small, he told me,—a wife, and a daughter about six,—and he wanted me to know them. Naturally we had become great friends. Very likely the man had saved my life, and he had done it without any act of heroism or daring, but simply by impressing me with the fact that his judgment was better than mine. I am apt to object to people of superior judgment, but Mr. Crowder was an exception to the ordinary superior person. From the way he talked it was plain that he had had much experience of various sorts, and that he had greatly advantaged thereby; but he gave himself no airs on this account, and there was nothing patronizing about him. If I were able to tell him anything he did not know—and I frequently was,—he was very glad to hear it.

Moreover, Mr. Crowder was a very good man to look at. He was certainly over fifty, and his closely trimmed hair was white, but he had a fresh and florid complexion. He was tall and well made, fashionably dressed, and had an erect and somewhat military carriage. He was fond of talking, and seemed fond of me, and these points in his disposition attracted me very much.

My relatives were few, they lived in the West, and I never had had a friend whose company was so agreeable to me as that of Mr. Crowder.

Mr. Crowder's residence was a handsome house in the upper part of the city. His wife was a slender lady, scarcely half his age, with a sweet and interesting face, and was attired plainly but tastefully. In general appearance she seemed to be the opposite of her husband in every way. She had suffered a week of anxiety, and was so rejoiced at having her husband again that when I met her, some hours after Crowder had reached the house, her glorified face seemed like that of an angel. But there was nothing demonstrative about her. Even in her great joy she was as quiet as a dove, and I was not surprised when her husband afterward told me that she was a Quaker.

I was entertained very handsomely by the Crowders. I spent several days with them, and although they were so happy to see each other, they made it very plain that they were also happy to have me with them, he because he liked me, she because he liked me.

On the day before my intended departure, Mr. Crowder and I were smoking, after dinner, in his study. He had been speaking of people and things that he had seen in various parts of the world, but after a time he became a little abstracted, and allowed me to do most of the talking.

"You must excuse me," he said suddenly, when I had repeated a question; "you must not think me willingly inattentive, but I was

"HIS WIFE WAS A SLENDER LADY."

considering something important—very important. Ever since you have been here,—almost ever since I have known you, I might say,—the desire has been growing upon me to tell you something known to no living being but myself."

This offer did not altogether please me; I had grown very fond of Crowder, but the confidences of friends are often very embarrassing. At this moment the study door was gently opened, and Mrs. Crowder came in.

"No," said she, addressing her husband with a smile; "thee need not let thy conscience trouble thee. I have not come to say anything about gentlemen being too long over their smoking. I only want to say that Mrs. Norris and two other ladies have just called, and I am going down to see them. They are a committee, and will not care for the society of gentlemen. I am sorry to lose any of your company, Mr. Randolph, especially as you insist that this is to be your last evening with us; but I do not think you would care anything about our ward organizations."

"Now, isn't that a wife to have!" exclaimed my host, as we resumed our cigars. "She thinks of everybody's happiness, and even wishes us to feel free to take another cigar if we desire it, although in her heart she disapproves of smoking."

We settled ourselves again to talk, and as there could be no objection to my listening to Crowder's confidences, I made none.

"What I have to tell you," he said presently, "concerns my life, present, past, and future. Pretty comprehensive, isn't it? I have long been looking for someone to whom I should be so drawn by bonds of sympathy that I should wish to tell him my story. Now, I feel that I am so drawn to you. The reason for this, in some degree at least, is because you believe in me. You are not weak, and it is my opinion that on important occasions you are very apt to judge for yourself, and not to care very much for the opinions of other people; and yet, on a most important occasion, you allowed me to judge for you. You are not only able to rely on yourself, but you know when it is right to rely on others. I believe you to be possessed of a fine and healthy sense of appreciation."

I laughed, and begged him not to bestow too many compliments upon me, for I was not used to them.

"I am not thinking of complimenting you," he said. "I am simply telling you what I think of you in order that you may understand why I tell you my story. I must first assure you, however, that I do not wish to place any embarrassing responsibility upon you by taking you into my confidence. All that I say to you, you may say to others when the time comes; but first I must tell the tale to you."

He sat up straight in his chair, and put down his cigar.

"I will begin," he said, "by stating that I am the Vizier of the Two-horned Alexander."

I sat up even straighter than my companion, and gazed steadfastly at him.

"No," said he, "I am not crazy. I expected you to think that, and am entirely prepared for your look of amazement and incipient horror. I will ask you, however, to set aside for a time the dictates of your own sense, and hear what I have to say. Then you can take the whole matter into consideration, and draw your own conclusions." He now leaned back in his chair, and went on with his story: "It would be more correct, perhaps, for me to say that I was the Vizier of the Two-horned Alexander, for that great personage died long ago. Now, I don't believe you ever heard anything about the Two-horned Alexander."

I had recovered sufficiently from my surprise to assure him that he was right.

My host nodded. "I thought so," said he; "very few people do know anything about that powerful potentate. He lived in the time of Abraham. He was a man of considerable culture, even of travel, and of an adventurous disposition. I entered into the service of his court when I was a very young man, and gradually I rose in position until I became his chief officer, or vizier."

I sprang from my chair. "Time of Abraham!" I exclaimed. "This is simply—"

"No, it is not," he interrupted, and speaking in perfect good humor. "I beg you will sit down and listen to me. What I have to say to you is not nearly so wonderful as the nature and power of electricity."

I obeyed; he had touched me on a tender spot, for I am an electrician, and can appreciate the wonderful.

"There has been a great deal of discussion," he continued, "in regard to the peculiar title given to Alexander, but the appellation two-horned has frequently been used in ancient times. You know Michelangelo gave two horns to Moses; but he misunderstood the tradition he had heard, and furnished the prophet with real horns. Alexander wore his hair arranged over his forehead in the shape of two protruding horns. This was simply a symbol of high authority; as the bull is monarch of the herd, so was he monarch among men. He was the first to use this symbol, although it was imitated afterward by various Eastern potentates.

"As I have said, Alexander was a man of enterprise, and it had come to his knowledge that there existed somewhere a certain spring the waters of which would confer immortality upon any descendant of Shem who should drink of them, and he started out to find this spring. I traveled with him for more than a year. It was on this journey that he visited Abraham when the latter was building the great edifice which the Mohammedans claim as their holy temple, the Kaaba.

"It was more than a month after we had parted from Abraham that I, being in advance of the rest of the company, noticed a little pool in the shade of a rock, and being very warm and thirsty, I got down on, my hands and knees, and putting my face to the water, drank of it. I drank heartily, and when I raised my head, I saw, to my amazement, that there was not a drop of water left in the spring. Now it so happened that when Alexander came to this spot, he stopped, and having regarded the little hollow under the rock, together with its surroundings, he dismounted and stood by it. He called me, and said: 'According to all the descriptions I have read, this might have been the spring of immortality for which I have been searching; but it cannot be such now, for there is no water in it.' Then he stooped down and looked carefully at the hollow. 'There has been water here,' said he, 'and that not long ago, for the ground is wet.'

"A horrible suspicion now seized upon me. Could I have drained the contents of the spring of inestimable value? Could I, without knowing it, have deprived my king of the great prize for which he had searched so long, with such labor and pains? Of course I was certain of nothing, but I bowed before Alexander, and told him that I had found an insignificant little puddle at the place, that I had tasted it and found it was nothing but common water, and in quantity so small that it scarcely sufficed to quench my thirst. If he would consent to camp in the shade, and wait a few hours, water would trickle again into the little basin, and fill it, and he could see for himself that this could not be the spring of which he was in search.

"We waited at that place for the rest of the day and the whole of the night, and the next morning the little basin was empty and entirely dry. Alexander did not, reproach me; he was accustomed to rule all men, even himself, and he forbade himself to think that

"'TIME OF ABRAHAM!' I EXCLAIMED."

I had interfered with the great object of his search. But he sent me home to his capital city, and continued his journey without me. 'Such a thirsty man must not travel with me,' he said. 'If we should really come to the immortal spring, he would be sure to drink it all.'

"Nine years afterward Alexander returned to his palace, and when I presented myself before him he regarded me steadfastly. I knew why he was looking at me, and I trembled. At length he spoke: 'Thou art not one day older than when I dismissed thee from my company. It was indeed the fountain of immortality which thou didst discover, and of which thou didst drink every drop. I have searched over the whole habitable world, and there is no other. Thou, too, art an aristocrat; thou, too, art of the family of Shem. It was for this reason that I placed thee near me, that I gave thee great power; and now thou hast destroyed all my hopes, my aspirations. Thou hast put an end to my ambitions. I had believed that I should rule the world, and rule it forever.' His face grew black; his voice was terrible. 'Retire!' he said. 'I will attend to thy future.'

"I retired, but my furious sovereign never saw me again. I was fifty-three years old when I drank the water in the little pool under the rock, and I was well aware that at the time of my sovereign's return I felt no older and looked no older. But still I hoped that this was merely the result of my general good health, and that when Alexander came back he would inform me that he had discovered the veritable spring of immortality; so I retained my high office, and waited. But I had made my plans for escape in case my hope should not be realized. In two minutes from the time I left his presence I had begun my flight, and there were no horses in all his dominions which could equal the speed of mine.

"Now began for me a long, long period of danger and terror, of concealment and deprivation. I fled into other lands, and these were conquered in order that I might be found. But at last Alexander died, and his son died, and the sons of his son died, and the whole story was forgotten or disbelieved, and I was no longer in danger of living forever as an example of the ingenious cruelty of an exasperated monarch.

"I do not intend to recount my life and adventures since that time; in fact, I shall scarcely touch upon them. You can see for yourself that that would be impossible. One might as well attempt to read a history of the world in a single evening. I merely want to say enough to make you understand the situation.

"A hundred years after I had fled from Alexander I was still fifty-three years old, and knew that that would be my age forever. I stayed so long in the place where I first established myself that people began to look upon me with suspicion. Seeing me grow no older, they thought I was a wizard, and I was obliged to seek a new habitation. Ever since, my fate has been the necessity of moving from place to place. I would go somewhere as a man beginning to show signs of age, and I would remain as long as a man could reasonably be supposed to live without becoming truly old and decrepit. Sometimes I remained in a place far longer than my prudence should have permitted, and many were the perils I escaped on account of this rashness; but I have gradually learned wisdom."

The man spoke so quietly and calmly, and made his statements in such a matter-of-fact way, that I listened to him with the same fascinated attention I had given to the theory of telegraphy without wires, when it was first propounded to me. In fact, I had been so influenced by his own conviction of the truth of what he said that I had been on the point of asking him if Abraham had really had anything to do with the building of the Islam temple, but had been checked by the thought of the utter absurdity of supposing that this man sitting in front of me could possibly know anything about it. But now I spoke. I did not want him to suppose that I believed anything he said, nor did I really intend to humor him in his insane retrospections; but what he had said suggested to me the very apropos remark that one might suppose he had been giving a new version of the story of the Wandering Jew.

At this he sat up very straight, on the extreme edge of his chair; his eyes sparkled. "You must excuse me," he said, "but for twenty seconds I am going to be angry. I can't help it. It isn't your fault, but that remark always enrages me. I expect it, of course, but it makes my blood boil, all the same."

"Then you have told your story before?" I said.

"Yes," he answered. "I have told it to certain persons to whom I thought it should be known. Some of these have believed it, some have not; but, believers or disbelievers, all have died and disappeared. Their opinions are nothing to me. You are now the only living being who knows my story." I was going to ask a question here, but he did not give me a chance. He was very much moved.

"I hate that Wandering Jew," said he, "or, I should say, I despise the thin film of a tradition from which he was constructed. There never was a Wandering Jew. There could not have been; it is impossible to conceive of a human being sent forth to wander in wretchedness forever. Moreover, suppose there had been such a man, what a poor, modern creature he would be compared with me! Even now he would be less than two thousand years old. You must excuse my perturbation, but I am sure that during the whole of the Christian-era I have never told my story to anyone who did not, in some way or other, make an absurd or irritating reference to the Wandering Jew. I have often thought, and I have no doubt

I am right, that the ancient story of my adventures as Kroudhr, the Vizier of the Two-horned Alexander, combined with what I have related, in one century or another, of my subsequent experiences, has given rise to the tradition of that very unpleasant Jew of whom Eugene Sue and many others have made good use. It is very natural that there should be legends about people who in some way or other are enabled to live forever. If Ponce de León and his companions had mysteriously disappeared when in search of the Fountain of Youth, there would be stories now about rejuvenated Spaniards wandering about the earth, and who would always continue to wander. But the Fountain of Youth is not a desirable water-supply, and a young person who should find such a pool would do well to wait until he had arrived at maturity before entering upon an existence of indefinite continuance.

"But I must go on with my story. At one time I made for myself a home, and remained in it for many, many years without making any change. I became a sort of hermit, and lived in a rocky cave. I allowed my hair and beard to grow, so that people really thought I was getting older—and older; at last I acquired the reputation of a prophet, and was held in veneration by a great many religious people. Of course I could not prophesy, but as I had such a vast deal of experience I was able to predicate intelligently something about the future from my knowledge of the past. I became famed as a wonderful seer, and there were a great many curious stories told about me.

"Among my visitors at that time was Moses. He had heard of me, and came to see what manner of man I was. We became very well acquainted. He was a man anxious to obtain information, and he asked me questions which embarrassed me very much; but I do not know that he suspected I had lived beyond the ordinary span of life. There are a good many traditions about this visit

"MOSES ASKED EMBARRASSING QUESTIONS."

of Moses, some of which are extant at the present day; but these, of course, are the result of what might be called cumulative imagination. Many of them are of Moslem origin, and the great Arabian historian Tabari has related some of them.

"I learned a great deal while I lived in this cave, both from scholars and from nature; but at last new generations arose who did not honor or even respect me, and by some I was looked upon as a fraudulent successor to the old prophet of whom their ancestors had told them, and so I thought it prudent to leave."

My interest in this man's extraordinary tissue of retrospection was increasing, and I felt that I must not doubt nor deny; to do so would be to break the spell, to close the book.

"Did it not sometimes fill you with horror to think that you must live forever?" I asked.

"Yes," he answered, "that has happened to me; but such feelings have long, long passed away. If you could have lived as I have, and had seen the world change from what it was when I was young to what it is now, you would understand how a man of my disposition, a man of my overpowering love of knowledge, love of discovery, love of improvement, love of progress of all kinds, would love to live. In fact, if I were now to be told that at the end of five thousand years I must expire and cease, it would fill me with gloom. Having seen so much, I expect more than most men are capable of comprehending. And I shall see it all — see the centuries unfold, behold the wonderful things of the future arise! The very thought of it fills me with inexpressible joy."

For a few moments he remained silent. I could understand the state of his mind, no matter how those mental conditions had been brought about.

"But you must not suppose," he continued, "that this earthly immortality is without its pains, its fears, I may say its horrors. It is precisely on account of all these that I am now talking to you. The knowledge that my life is always safe, no matter in what peril I may be, does not relieve me from anxiety and apprehension of evil. It would be a curse to live if I were not in sound physical condition; it would be a curse to live as a slave; it would be a curse to live in a dungeon. I have known vicissitudes and hardships of every kind, but I have been fortunate enough to preserve myself whole and unscathed, in spite of the dangers I have incurred.

"I often think from what a terrible fate I saved my master, Alexander of the two horns. If he had found the fountain he might have enjoyed his power and dominion for a few generations. Then he would have been thrown down, cast out, and even if he had escaped miseries which I cannot bear to mention, he never could have regained his high throne. He would have been condemned to live forever in a station for which he was not fitted.

"It is very different with me. My nature allows me to adapt myself to various conditions, and my habits of prudence prevent me from seeking to occupy any position which may be dangerous to me by making me conspicuous, and from which I could not easily retire when I believe the time has come to do so. I have been almost everything; I have even been a soldier. But I have never taken up arms except when obliged to do so, and I have known as little of war as possible. No weapon or missile could kill me, but I have a great regard for my arms and legs. I have been a ruler of men, but I have trembled in my high estate, for I feared the populace. They could do everything except take my life. Therefore, I made it a point to abdicate when the skies were clear. In such cases I set out on journeys from which I never returned.

"I have also lived the life of the lowly; I have drawn water, and I have hewn wood. By the way, that reminds me of a little incident which may interest you. I was employed in the East India House

AN ENCOUNTER WITH CHARLES LAMB.

at the time Charles Lamb was a clerk there. It was not long after he had begun to contribute his Elia essays to the London Magazine. I had read some of them, and was interested in the man. I met him several times in the corridors or on the stairways, and one day I was going up stairs, carrying a hod of coals, as he was coming down. Looking up at him, I made a misstep, and came near dropping a portion of my burden. 'My good man,' said he, with a queer smile, 'if you would learn to carry your coals as well as you carry your age you would do well.' I don't remember what I said in reply; but I know I thought if Charles Lamb could be made aware of my real age, he would abandon his Elia work and devote himself to me."

"It is a pity you did not tell him," I suggested.

"No," replied my host. "He might have been interested, but he could not have appreciated the situation, even if I had told him everything. He would not really have known my age, for he would not have believed me. I might have found myself in a lunatic asylum. I never saw Lamb again, and very soon after that meeting I came to America."

Chapter Two

"Here Are Two Points about your story that I do not comprehend," said I (and as I spoke I could not help the thought that in reality I did not comprehend any of it). "In the first place, I don't see how you could live for a generation or two in one place and then go off to an entirely new locality. I should think there were not enough inhabited spots in the world to accommodate you in such extensive changes."

Mr. Crowder smiled. "I don't wonder you ask that question," he said; "but in fact it was not always necessary for me to seek new places. There are towns in which I have taken up my residence many times. But as I arrived each time as a stranger from afar, and as these sojourns were separated by many years, there was no one to suppose me to be a person who had lived in that place a century or two before."

"Then you never had your portrait painted," I remarked.

"Oh, yes, I have," he replied. "Toward the close of the thirteenth century I was living in Florence, being at that time married to a lady of wealthy family, and she insisted upon my having my portrait painted by Cimabue, who, as you know, was the master of Giotto. After my wife's death I departed from Florence, leaving behind me the impression that I intended soon to return; and I would have been glad to take the portrait with me, but I had no opportunity. It was in 1503 that I went back to Florence, and as soon as I could I visited the stately mansion where I, had once lived, and there in the gallery still hung the portrait. This was an unsatisfactory discovery, for I might wish at some future time to settle again in Florence, and I had hoped that the portrait had faded, or that it had been destroyed; but Cimabue painted too well, and his work was then held in high value, without regard to his subject. Finding myself entirely alone in the gallery, I cut that picture from its frame. I concealed it under my cloak, and when I reached my lodging, I utterly destroyed it. I did not feel that I was committing any crime in doing this; I had ordered and paid for the painting, and I felt that I had a right to do what I pleased with it."

"I don't see how you can help having your picture taken in these days," I said; "even if you refuse to go to a photographer's, you can't escape the Kodak people. You have a striking presence."

"Oh, I can't get away from photographers," he answered. "I have had a number of pictures taken, at the request of my wife and other people. It is impossible to avoid it, and that is one of the reasons why I am now telling you my story. What is the other point about which you wished to ask me?"

"I cannot comprehend," I answered, "how you should ever have found yourself poor and obliged to work. I should say that a man who had lived so long would have accumulated, in one way or another, immense wealth, inexhaustible treasures."

"Oh, yes," said he, with a smile, "Monte Cristo, and all that sort of thing. Your notion is a perfectly natural one, but I assure you, Mr. Randolph, that it is founded upon a mistake. Over and over and over again I have amassed wealth; but I have not been able to retain it permanently, and often I have suffered for the very necessaries of life. I have been hungry, knowing that I could never starve. The explanation of this state of things is simple enough: I would trade; I would speculate; I would marry an heiress; I would become rich; for many years I would enjoy my possessions. Then the time would come when people said: 'Who owns these houses?''To whom belongs this money in the banks?' 'These properties were purchased in our great-grandfathers' times; the accounts in the banks were opened long before our oldest citizens were born. Who is it then that is making out leases and drawing checks?' I have employed all sorts of subterfuges in order to retain my property, but I have always found that to prove my continued identity I should have to acknowledge my immortality; and in that case, of course, I should have been adjudged a lunatic, and everything would have been taken from me. So I generally managed, before the time arrived when it was actually necessary for me to do so, to turn my property, as far as possible, into money, and establish myself in some other place as a stranger. But there were times when I was obliged to hurry from my home and take nothing with me. Then I knew misery.

"It was during the period of one of my greatest depressions that I met with a monk who was afterward St. Bruno, and I joined, the Carthusian monastery which he founded in Calabria. In the midst of their asceticism, their seclusion, and their silence I hoped that I might be asked no questions, and need tell no lies; I hoped that I might be allowed to live as long as I pleased without disturbance: but I found no such immunity. When Bruno died, and his successor had followed him into the grave, it was proposed that I should be the next prior; but this would not have suited me at all. I had employed all my time in engrossing books, but the duties of a prior were not for me, so I escaped, and went out into the world again."

As I sat and listened to Mr. Crowder, his story seemed equally

"'I CUT THAT PICTURE FROM ITS FRAME.'"

wonderful to me, whether it were a plain statement of facts or the relation of an insane dream. It was not a wild tale, uttered in the enthusiastic excitement of a disordered mind; but it was a series of reminiscences, told quietly and calmly, here a little, there a little, without chronological order, each one touched upon as it happened to suggest itself. From wondering I found myself every now and then believing: but—whenever I realized the folly in which I was indulging myself, I shook off my credulity and endeavored to listen with interest, but without judgment, for in this way only could I most thoroughly enjoy the strange narrative; but my lapses into unconscious belief were frequent.

"You have spoken of marriage," said I. "Have you had many wives?"

My host leaned back in his chair and looked up at the ceiling. "That is a subject," he said, "of which I think as little as I can, and yet I must speak to you of it. It is right that I should do so. I have been married so often that I can scarcely count the wives I have had. Beautiful women, good women, some of them women to whom I would have given immortality had I been able; but they died, and died, and died. And here is one of the great drawbacks of living forever. Yet it was not always the death of my wives which saddened me the most; it was their power of growing old. I would marry a young woman, beautiful, charming. You need not be surprised that I was able to do this, for in all ages woman has been in the habit of disregarding the years of man, and I have always had a youthful spirit; I think it is Daudet who says that the most dangerous lover is the man of fifty-three. I would live happily with a wife; she would gradually grow to be the same age as myself; and then she would become older and older, and I did not. As I have said, there were women to whom I would have given immortality if I could; but I will add that there have been times when I would have given up my own immortality to be able to pass gently into old age with a beloved wife.

"You will want to know if I have had descendants. They exist by the thousand; but if you ask me where they are, I must tell you that I do not know. I now have but one child, a little girl who is asleep upstairs. I have gathered around me families of sons and daughters; they have grown up, married, and my grandchildren have sat upon my knees. Sometimes, at long intervals, I have known great-grandchildren. But when my sons and daughters have grown gray and gone to their graves, I have withdrawn myself from the younger people, — some of whom were not acquainted with me, others even had never heard of me,—and then by the next generation the old ancestor, if remembered at all, was connected only with the distant past. And so family after family have melted into the great mass of human beings, and are as completely lost as though they were water thrown into the sea.

"I have always been fond of beautiful women, and as you have met Mrs. Crowder, you know that my disposition has not changed. Sarah, the wife of Abraham, was considered a woman of great beauty in her day, and the fame of her charms continues; but I assure you that if she lived now her attractions would not have given her husband so much trouble. I saw a good deal of Sarah when I visited Abraham with my master Alexander, and I have seen many more beautiful women since that time. Hagar was a fine woman, but she was too dark, and her face had an anxious expression which interfered with her beauty."

"Was Hagar really the wife of Abraham," I asked, "as the Mussulmans say, and was Ishmael considered his heir?"

"When I saw them," my host continued, "the two women seemed as friendly as sisters, and Isaac was not yet born. At that time it was considered, of course, that Ishmael was Abraham's heir. Certainly he was a much finer man than Isaac, with whom I became acquainted a long time afterward. There were some very beautiful women at the court of Solomon, and one of these was Balkis, the famous Queen of Sheba."

"Did you ever meet Cleopatra?" I interrupted.

"I never saw her," was the answer, "but, from what I have heard, I do not think I should have cared for her if I had seen her asleep. What might have happened had I seen her awake is quite another matter. I have noticed that women grow more beautiful as the world grows older, and men grow taller and better developed. You would consider me, I think, a man of average size; but I tell you that in my early life I was exceptionally tall, and I have no doubt it was my stature and presence to which I largely owed my preferment at the court of Alexander. I was living in Spain toward the close of the tenth century, when I married the daughter of an Arabian physician, who was a wonderfully beautiful woman. She was not dark, like the ordinary Moorish women. In feature and form she surpassed any creation of the Greek sculptors, and I have been in many of their workshops, and have seen their models. This lady lived longer than any other wife I had. She lived so long, in fact, that when we left Cordova we both thought it well that she should pass as my mother. She was one of the few wives to whom I told my story. It did not shock her, for she believed her father to be a miracle-worker, and she had faith in many strange things. Her great desire was to live as long as I should, and I think she believed that this might happen. She died at the age of one hundred and fifteen, and was lively and animated to the very last. My first American wife was a fine woman, too. She was a French creole, and died fifteen years ago. We had no children."

"It strikes me," I said suddenly, "that you must understand a great many languages—you speak so much of living with people of different nations."

"It would be impossible," he answered, "unless I were void of ordinary intelligence, to live as long as I have, and not become a general linguist. Of course I had to learn the languages of the countries I visited, and as I was always a student, it delighted me to do so. In fact, I not only studied, but I wrote. When the Alexandrian library was destroyed, fourteen of my books were burned. When I was in Italy with my first American wife, I visited the museum at Naples, and in the room where the experts were unrolling the papyri found in Pompeii, I looked over the shoulder of one of them, and, to my amazement, found that one of the rolls was an account-book of my own. I had been a broker in Pompeii, and these were the records of moneys I had loaned, on interest, to various merchants and tradespeople. I was always fond of dealing in money, and at present I am a broker in Wall street. During the first crusades I was a banker in Genoa, and lent large sums to the noble knights who were setting forth for Jerusalem."

"Was much of it repaid?" I asked.

"Most of it. The loans were almost always secured by good property. As I look back upon the vast panorama of my life," my host continued, after a pause, "I most pleasantly recall my various intimacies with learned men, and my own studies and researches; but in the great company of men of knowledge whom I have known, there was not one in whom I was so much interested as in King Solomon. I visited his court because I greatly wished to know a man who knew so much. It was not difficult to obtain access to him, for I came as a stranger from Ethiopia, to the east of the Red Sea, and the king was always anxious to see intelligent people from foreign parts. I was able to tell him a good deal which he did not know, and he became fond of my society.

"'WHEN WE LEFT CORDOVA.'"

"I found Solomon a very well-informed man. He had not read and studied books as much as I had, and he had not had my advantages of direct intercourse with learned men; but he was a most earnest and indefatigable student of nature. I believe he knew more about natural history than any human being then living, or who had preceded him. Whenever it was possible for him to do so, he studied animal nature from the living model, and all the beasts, birds, and fishes which it was possible for him to obtain alive were quartered in the grounds of his palace. In a certain way he was an animal-tamer. You may well imagine that this great king's wonderful possessions, as well as the man himself, were the source of continual delight to me.

"The time-honored story of Solomon's carpet on which he mounted and was wafted away to any place, with his retinue, had a good deal of foundation in fact; for Solomon was an exceedingly ingenious man, and not only constructed parachutes by which people could safely descend from great heights, but he made some attempts in the direction of ballooning. I have seen small bags of thin silk, covered with a fine varnish made of gum to render them air-tight, which, being inflated with hot air and properly ballasted, rose high above the earth, and were wafted out of sight by the wind. Many people supposed that in the course of time Solomon would be able to travel through the air, and from this idea was derived the tradition that he really did so.

"Another of the interesting legends regarding King Solomon concerned his dominion over the Jinns. These people, of whom so much has been written and handed down by word of mouth, and who were supposed by subsequent generations to be a race of servile demons, were, in reality, savage natives of surrounding countries, who were forced by the king to work on his great buildings and other enterprises, and who occupied very much the position of the coolies of the present day. But that story of the dead Solomon and the Jinns who were at work on the temple gives a good idea of one of the most important characteristics of this great ruler. He was a man who gave personal attention to all his affairs, and was in the habit of overseeing the laborers on his public works. Do you remember the story to which I refer?"

I was obliged to say that I did not think I had ever heard it.

"The story runs thus," said my host "The Jinns were at work building the temple, and Solomon, according to his custom, overlooked them daily. At the time when the temple was nearly completed Solomon felt that his strength was passing from him, and that he would not have much longer to live. This greatly troubled him, for he knew that when the Jinns should find that his watchful eye would be no more upon them, they would rebel and refuse to work, and the temple would not be finished during his reign. Therefore, as the story runs, he came, one day, into the temple, and hoped that he might be enabled to remain there until the great edifice should be finished. He stood leaning on his staff, and the Jinns, when they beheld their master, continued to work, and work, and work. When night came Solomon still remained standing in his accustomed place, and the Jinns worked on, afraid to cease their toil for a moment.

"Standing thus, Solomon died; but the Jinns did not know it, and their toil and labor continued, by night and by day. Now, according to the tradition, a little white ant, one of the kind which devours wood, came up out of the earth on the very day on which Solomon died, and began to gnaw the inside of his staff. She gnawed a little every day, until at last the staff became hollow from one end to the other; and on the day when she finished her work, the work of the Jinns was also finished. Then the staff crumbled, and the dead Solomon fell, face foremost, to the earth. The

“‘I HAD BEEN A BROKER IN POMPEII.’”

Jinns, perceiving that they had been slaving day and night for a master who was dead, fled away with yells of rage and vexation. But the glorious temple was finished, and King Solomon's work was done. Tabari tells this story, and it is also found in the Koran; but the origin of it was nothing more than the well-known custom of Solomon to exercise personal supervision over those who were working for him.

"I was the person from whom Solomon first heard of the Queen of Sheba. I had lived in her capital city for several years, and she had summoned me before her, and had inquired about the places I had visited and the things I had seen. What I said about this wonderful woman and the admirable administration of her empire interested Solomon very much, and he was never tired of hearing me talk about her. At one time I believe he thought of sending me as an ambassador to her, but afterward gave up this notion, as I did not possess the rank or position which would have qualified me to represent him and his court; so he sent a suitable delegation, and, after a great deal of negotiation and diplomatic by-play, the queen actually determined to come to see Solomon. Soon after her arrival with her great retinue, she saw me, and immediately recognized me, and the first thing she said to me was that she perceived I had grown a good deal older than when I had been living in her domains. This delighted me, for before coming to Jerusalem I had allowed my hair and beard to grow, and had dispensed with as much as possible of my ordinary erect mien and lightness of step; for I was very much afraid, if I were not careful, that the wise king would find out that there was something irregular in my longevity, and an old man may continue to look old much longer than a middle-aged man can continue to appear middle-aged.

"It was a great advantage to me to find myself admitted to a certain intimacy with both the king and his visitor the queen. As I was a subject of neither of them, they seemed to think this circumstance allowed a little more familiarity than otherwise they would have shown. Besides, my age had a great deal to do with the freedom with which they spoke to me. Each of them seemed anxious to know everything I could tell about the other, and I would sometimes be subjected to embarrassing questions.

"There is a great deal of extravagance and perversion in the historical and traditional accounts of the tricks which these two royal personages played upon each other. Most of these old stories are too silly to repeat, but some of them had foundation in fact. They tell a tale of how the queen set five hundred boys and five hundred girls before the king, all the girls dressed as boys and all the boys dressed as girls, and then she asked him, as he was such a wise man, immediately to distinguish those of one sex from those of the other. Solomon did not hesitate a moment, but ordering basins of water to be brought, he commanded the young people to wash their hands. Thereupon he watched them closely, and as the boys washed only their hands, while the girls rolled up their sleeves and washed their arms as well as their hands, Solomon was able, without any trouble, to pick out the one from the other. Now, something of this kind really happened, but there were only ten boys and ten girls. But in the course of ages the story grew, and the whole thing was made absurd; for there never was a king in the world, nor would there be likely to be one, who could have a thousand basins ready immediately to put before a company who wished to wash their hands. But the result of this scheme convinced the queen that Solomon was a man of the deepest insight into the manners and, customs of human beings, as well as those of animals, birds, and fishes.

"But there is an incident with which I was personally connected

SOLOMON AND THE JINNS.

which was known at the time to very few people, and was never publicly related. The beautiful queen desired, above all other things, to know whether Solomon held her in such high esteem because she was a mighty queen, or on account of her personal attractions; and in order to discover the truth in regard to this question, she devised a little scheme to which she made me a party. There was a young woman in her train, of surpassing beauty, whose name was Liridi, and the queen was sure that Solomon had never seen her, for it was her custom to keep her most beautiful attendants in the background. This maiden the queen caused to be dressed in the richest and most becoming robes, and adorned her, besides, with jewels and golden ornaments, which set off her beauty in an amazing manner. Then, having made many inquiries of me in regard to the habits of Solomon, she ordered Liridi to walk alone in one of the broad paths of the royal gardens at the time when the king was wont to stroll there by himself. The queen wished to find out whether this charming apparition would cause the king to forget her for a time, and she ordered me to be in the garden, and so arrange my rambles that I could, without being observed, notice what happened when the king should meet Liridi. I was on hand before the appointed time, and when I saw, the girl walking slowly up the shaded avenue, I felt obliged to go to her and tell her that she was too soon, and that she must not meet Solomon near the palace. As I spoke to her I was amazed at her wonderful beauty, and I did not believe it possible that the king could gaze upon her without such emotion as would make him forget for the moment every other woman in the world.

"The queen had purposely made an appointment with him for the same hour, so that if he did not come she would know what was detaining him. At length Solomon appeared at the far end of the avenue, and Liridi began again her pensive stroll. When the king reached her, she retired to one side, her head bowed, as if she had not expected to meet royalty in this secluded spot. King Solomon was deep in thought as he walked, but when he came near the maiden, he raised his eyes and suddenly stopped. I was nearby, behind some shrubbery, and it was plain enough to me that he was dazzled by this lovely apparition. He asked her who she was, and when she had told him he gazed at her with still greater attention. Then suddenly he laughed aloud. 'Go tell the queen,' said he, 'that she hath missed her mark. The arrow which is adorned with golden trappings and precious stones cannot fly aright.' Then he went on, still laughing to himself. In the evening he told me about this incident, and said that if the maiden had been arrayed in the simple robes which became her station he would have suspected nothing, and would probably have stopped to converse with her so long that he would have failed to keep his appointment with his royal guest.

"The queen was very much annoyed at the ill success of her little artifice, but it was not long after this that she and the king discovered their true feeling for each other, and they were soon married. The wedding was a grand one—grander than tradition relates, grander than the modern mind can easily comprehend. When they went to the palace to sit for the first time in state before the vast assembly of dignitaries and courtiers, the queen found, beside the throne of Solomon, her own throne, which he had caused to be brought from Sheba in time for this occasion. This incident, I think, affected her more agreeably than anything else that happened. Great were the festivities. Honors and dignities were bestowed on every hand, and I might have come in for some substantial benefit had it not been that I committed a great blunder. I had fallen in love with the beautiful Liridi, and as the

"'GO TELL THE QUEEN.'"

queen seemed so gracious and kind to everybody, I made bold to go to her and ask that she would allow me to marry her charming handmaiden. But, to my surprise, this request angered the queen. She told me that such an old man as myself ought to be ashamed to take a young girl to wife; that she was opposed to such marriages; and that, in fact, I ought to be punished for even mentioning the subject.

"I retired in disgrace, and very soon afterward I left Jerusalem, for I have found, by varied experiences, that the displeasure of rulers is an unhealthful atmosphere in which to live. However, the Queen of Sheba did not get altogether the better of me. As you know, King Solomon and his royal wife did not reign together very long. They ruled over two great kingdoms, each of which required the presence of its sovereign; so Queen Balkis soon went back to Sheba with more wealth, more soldiers, more camels, horses, and grand surroundings of every kind, than she had brought with her. She carried in her baggage-train her royal throne, but she did not take with her the beautiful Liridi. That lady had been given in marriage to an officer in Solomon's army, and thirty years afterward, in the land of Asshur, where her father was stationed, I married the youngest daughter of Liridi. The latter was then dead, but my wife, with whom I lived happily for many years in Phoenicia, was quite as beautiful. I was greatly inclined, at the time, to send a courier with a letter to the Queen of Sheba, informing her of what had happened; but I was afraid. She was then an elderly woman, and I was informed that age had actually sharpened her wits, so that if I had incensed her and given her reason to suspect the truth about my unnatural age, I believe there was no known country in which I could have concealed myself from her emissaries.

"There are many, many incidents which, crowd upon my

memory," continued my host, "but—" and as he spoke he pulled out his watch. "My conscience!" he exclaimed, "it is twenty minutes past three! I should be ashamed of myself, Mr. Randolph, for having kept you up so long."

We both rose to our feet, and I was about to say something polite, suited to the occasion, but he gave me no chance.

"I felt I must talk to you," he said, speaking very rapidly. "I have discovered you to be a man of appreciation—a man who should hear my story. I have felt for some years that it would soon become impossible for me to conceal my experiences from my fellowmen. I believe mankind has now reached a stage of enlightenment—at least, in this country—when the person who makes strange discoveries which cannot be explained, and the person who announces facts which cannot be comprehended by the human mind, need not fear to be punished as a sorcerer, or thrust into a cell as a lunatic. I may be mistaken in regard to this latter point, but I think I am right. In any case, I do not wish to live much longer as I have been living. As I must live on, with generation after generation rising up about me, I want those generations to know before they depart from this earth that I am a person who does not die. I am tired of deceptions; I am tired of leaving the places where I have lived long and am known, and arriving in other places where I am a stranger, and where I must begin my life again.

"I do not wish to be in a hurry to make my revelations to the world at large. I do not wish to startle people without being able to show them proof of what I say. I wish to speak only to persons who are worthy to hear my story, and I have begun with you. I do not want you to believe me until you are quite ready to do so. Think over what I have said, consider it carefully, and make up your mind slowly.

"You are a young man in good health, and you will, in all probability, live long enough to assure yourself of the truth or falsity of what I have told you about my indefinite longevity. I should be glad to relate my story to scientific men, to physicians, to students; but, as I have said, we shall wait for that. In the meantime, you may, if you choose, write down what I have told you, or as much of it as you remember. I have no written records of my past life. Long, long ago I made such, but I destroyed them, for I knew not what evil they might bring upon me were they discovered. But you may write the little I have told you, and when you feel that the time has come, you may give it to the world. And now we must retire. It is wrong to keep you out of your bed any longer."

"One word," said I. "Do you intend now to tell your wife?"

"Yes," he answered, "I shall tell her tomorrow. Having reposed confidence in you, it would be treating her shamefully if I should withhold that confidence from her. She has often said to me that I do not look a day older than when I married her. I want her now to know that I need never look a day older; I shall counterfeit old age no more."

I did not sleep well during what was left of the night, for my mind went traveling backward and forward through the ages. The next morning, at breakfast, Mr. Crowder appeared in his ordinary good spirits, but his wife was very quiet. She was pale, and occasionally I thought I saw signs of trouble on her usually placid brow. I felt sure that he had told her his story. As I looked at her, I could not prevent myself from seriously wondering that a man who had seen Abraham and Sarah, and had been personally acquainted with the Queen of Sheba, should now be married to a Quaker lady from North Sixteenth street, Philadelphia.

After breakfast she found an opportunity of speaking to me privately.

"Do you believe," she asked very hurriedly, "what my husband told you last night—the story of his earthly immortality?"

"I really do not know," I answered, "whether I believe it or not. My reason assures me that it is impossible; and yet there is in Mr. Crowder's manner so much sincerity, so much—"

Contrary to her usual habits, I am sure, she interrupted me.

"Excuse me," she said, "but I must speak while I have the chance. You must believe what my husband has said to you. He has told me everything, and I know that it is impossible for him to tell a lie. I have not yet arranged my ideas in regard to this wonderful revelation, but I believe. If the time should ever come when I shall know I should not believe, that will be another matter. But he is my husband. I know him, I trust him. Will you not do the same?"

"I will do it," I exclaimed, "until the time comes when I shall know that I cannot possibly do so."

She gave me her hand, and I shook it heartily.

"SHE GAVE ME HER HAND, AND I SHOOK IT HEARTILY."

Chapter Three

About four months after my first acquaintance with Mr. and Mrs. Crowder, I found myself again in New York; and when I called at the house of my friends, I received from them a most earnest invitation to take up my abode with them during my stay in the great city.

Of course, this invitation was eagerly accepted; for not only was the Crowder house a home of the most charming hospitality, but my interest in the extraordinary man who was evidently so glad to be my host was such that not one day had passed since I last saw him in which I did not think of him, and consider his marvelous statements from every point of view which my judgment was capable of commanding. I found Mr. Crowder unchanged in appearance and manner, and his wife was the same charming young woman I had known. But there was nothing surprising in this. People generally do not change very much in four months; and yet, in talking to Mr. Crowder, I could not prevent myself from earnestly scanning his features to see if he had grown any older. He noticed this, and laughed heartily.

"It is natural enough," he said, "that you should wish to assure yourself that there is a good foundation to your belief in what I have told you; but you are in too great a hurry: you must wait some years for that sort of proof, one way or the other. But I believe that you do believe me, and I am not in the least disturbed by the way you look at me."

After dinner, on the first day of my visit, when we were smoking together, I asked Mr. Crowder if he would not continue the recital of his experiences, which were of such absorbing interest to me that sometimes I found them occupying my mind to an extent which excluded the consideration of everything relating to myself and the present time.

"From one point of view," he said, "that would be a bad thing for you: but I don't look at it in that way; in fact, I hope you may become my biographer. I will furnish you with material enough, and you can arrange it and put it in shape; that is, if, in the course of a few years, you consider that, in doing what I ask of you, you will be writing the true life of a man, and not a collection of fanciful stories. So I hope you may find that you have not lost your time when thinking so much of a man of the past."

Now, there is no doubt that I did most thoroughly believe in Crowder. I had argued with myself against this belief to the utmost extent of my ability, and I had now given up the effort. If I should disbelieve him I would deprive myself of one of the most precious privileges of my existence, and I did not intend to do so until I found myself absolutely forced to admit that I was mistaken. Time would settle all this, and all that I had to do now was to listen, enjoy, and be thankful for the opportunity.

"I am not going to tell any stories now," he said, "for my wife has not overcome her dislike to tobacco smoke, and she has insisted that she shall be one of my hearers when I tell stories of my past life to you; but I can tell you this, my friend: she will believe every word I say; there can be no possible doubt of that. I have told her a good many things since I saw you last, and her faith in me is a joy unspeakable."

Of course I was delighted to hear that this charming lady was to be my fellow auditor, and said so.

"I often think of you two," said Mr. Crowder, contemplatively leaning back in his armchair. "I think of you together, but I am bound to say that the thought is not altogether pleasant." I showed my amazement at this remark. "It can't be helped," he said; "it can't be helped. It's one of the things I have to suffer. I have suffered it over and over again thousands of times, but I never get used to it. Here you are, two young people, young enough to be my children: one is my wife; the other, I am proud to say, my best friend. You are the only persons in the world who know my story. You have faith in me, and the thought of that faith is the greatest pleasure of my life. Year by year you two will grow older; year by year you will more nearly approach my own age, and become, according to the ordinary opinion of the world, more suitable companions for me. Then you will reach my age. We shall be three gray-haired friends. Then will come the saddening time, the mournful days. You two will grow older and older, and I shall remain where I am—always fifty-three. Then you will grow to be elderly—elderly people; at last, aged people. If you live long enough I shall look up to you as I would to my parents."

This was a state of things I had never contemplated. I could scarcely appreciate it. "Of course," he continued, "I wish you both to live long; but don't you see how it affects me? But enough of that. Here comes Mrs. Crowder, and with her all subjects must be pleasant ones."

"I think thee must buy some short cigars," she said, just putting her head inside the door, "to smoke after dinner. If large ones are necessary, they can be smoked after I go to bed. I am getting very impatient; for now that Mr. Randolph is here, I believe that thee is going to be unusually interesting."

We arose immediately, and joined Mrs. Crowder in the library.

This lady's use of the plain speech customary with Quakers was very pleasant to me. I had had but little acquaintance with it, and at first its independence of grammatical rules struck upon me unpleasantly; but I soon began to enjoy Mrs. Crowder's speech, when she was addressing her husband, much more than I did the remarks she made to me, the latter being always couched in the most correct English. There was a sweetness about her "thee" which had the quality of gentle music; and when she used the word "thy" it was pronounced so much like "thee" that I could scarcely perceive the difference. To her husband and child she always used the Quaker speech of the present day; and as I did not like being set aside in this way, I said to her that I hoped there was no rule of the Society of Friends which would compel her to make a change in her form of speech when she addressed me. "If thee likes," she said, with a smile, "thee is welcome to all the plain speech thee wants." And after that, when she spoke to me, she did not turn me out among the world's people.

"Now, you know," said Mr. Crowder, "that I'm not going to play the part of an historian. That sort of discourse would bore me, and it would bore you. If there is any kind of thing that you would like to hear about, all you have to do is to ask me; and if you don't care to do this, I will tell you whatever comes up in my memory, without any regard to chronology or geography, just as I talked to you before. If I were to begin at the beginning and go straight along, even if I skipped ever so much, the story would—it would be a great deal too long."

I am sure that Mrs. Crowder and I both felt what he did not wish to say—that we were not likely to live to hear it all.

"There are a great many things I should like to ask thee," said Mrs. Crowder, speaking quickly, as if to change the subject of her thoughts; "but I believe I have forgotten most of them. But here is something I should like to know—that is," she said, turning to me, "if thee hasn't anything in thy mind which thee wishes to ask about?"

I noticed that she pronounced "thy" very distinctly, a little bit of grammatical conscience probably obtruding itself. Of course I had nothing to ask, and she put her question: "What *did* thee do in the dark ages?"

Crowder laughed. "That is a big question," said he, "and the only answer I can give you in a general way is that there were so many things that I was not able to do, or did not dare to do, that I look upon those centuries as the most disagreeable part of my whole life. But you must not suppose that everybody felt as I did. A great many of the people by whom I was surrounded at that doleful period appeared to be happier and better satisfied with their circumstances than any I have known before or after. There was little ambition, less responsibility; and if the poor and weak suffered from the rapacity and violence of the rich and strong, they accepted their misfortunes as if they were something they were bound to expect, such as bad weather. I am not going to talk history, and there is one thing that your question reminds me of. During that portion of the middle ages which is designated as dark, I employed myself in a great many different ways: I was laborer, sailor, teacher, and I cannot tell you what besides; but more frequently than anything else I was a teacher."

"Thee must have been an angel of light," Mrs. Crowder remarked.

"No," said he; "an angel of light would have been very conspicuous in those days. I didn't pose for such a part. In fact, if I had not succeeded in appearing like a partial ignoramus I should have been obliged to go into a monastery, for in those days the monks were the only people who knew anything. They expected to do all the teaching that was done; but, for all that, a few scholars cropped up now and then, and here and there, who did not care to have monks for masters; and by instructing these in a very modest, quiet way I frequently managed to make a living."

"I should think," I said, "that at any time and in any period you would have been a person of importance, with your experience and knowledge of men."

Mr. Crowder shook his head. "No," said he; "not so. To make myself of importance in that time I must have been a soldier, and the profession of arms, you know, is one I have always avoided. A man who cannot be killed should take great care that he is not wounded."

"I am so glad that thee did take care," ejaculated Mrs. Crowder; "but even I cannot see how thee kept out of fighting in those disorderly times."

"I did not keep out of it altogether, but in every possible way I tried to do so, and for the most part succeeded. Whenever I was likely to be involved in military operations, I let my hair and beard grow, and the white-haired old man was usually exempted. I have had far more experience in keeping out of battles than any other human being has had in the art of winning them. But what you two want is a story, and I will give you one.

"During some of the earlier years of the seventh century, I was living in Ravenna, and there I had three or four scholars whom I taught occasionally. I did not dare to keep a regular school, with fixed hours and all that; but while I was not working at my trade, which was then that of a mason, I gave lessons to some young people in the neighborhood. Sometimes I taught in the evening, sometimes in bad weather when we did not work out of doors. Not one of my scholars showed any intelligence, except a girl about eighteen years old. Her father, I think, was a professional robber, for his family lived very well, and he was generally absent from home at the head of a little band of desperate fellows, of whom there were a great many in that region.

"This girl, whose name was Rina, had an earnest desire for knowledge, and showed a great capacity for imbibing it and retaining it. In fact, I believe she was the most intelligent person in that region."

"Was she pretty?" asked Mrs. Crowder.

"Yes," replied her husband; "she was very good-looking. I was so interested in her desire for knowledge that I taught her a great deal more than I would have dared to teach anybody else; and the more I taught, the more she wanted to learn.

"I soon became very much concerned about Rina. Some man of the neighborhood, old or young, would be sure to marry her before very long, and then there would be an end of the development of what I considered the brightest intellect of the day."

"So to keep that from happening to her, thee married her thyself?" asked Mrs. Crowder.

Her husband smiled. "Yes; that is what I did. You know," he said, addressing me, "that I believe that Mrs. Crowder takes more interest, in my marriages than in anything else I have done in the course of my career."

"Certainly I do," she said, with a little flush. "Of course thee had to be married, and it is natural enough that I should want to know whom thee married, and all about it."

"Well," said Mr. Crowder, "we must get on with this. A priest with whom I was acquainted married us, and we immediately fled from Ravenna. After a year or two of wandering through benighted countries where even kings and rulers could not write their names, and where reading seemed to be a lost art, except in the monasteries, we made up our minds, if possible, we would go from darkness into light, and so we set out on a journey to China."

At this statement Mrs. Crowder and I looked surprised.

"I don't wonder you open your eyes," said he. "It must seem odd to you, unless you are very familiar with the history of the period, that we should go from Europe to China in search of enlightenment and civilization; but that is what we did, and we found what we looked for. As the Pope had sent an envoy to China, and as some Nestorian missionaries had gone there, I believed that we could go.

"This journey to the Chinese province of Nan-hae occupied the greater part of five years; but to me personally that was of no account, for I had time enough. Although we passed through all sorts of hardships and dangers, my wife was greatly interested in the strange things and people she met. Sometimes we traveled by water, sometimes on horses and asses, and very often we walked. During the last part of the journey we joined a caravan which went through central Asia.

"At that time China was ruled by a woman, the Empress Woo. For a long time back there had been a period of great intellectual activity in China. Literature and the arts flourished, and while the great personages of Europe did not know how to write, these people were printing from wooden blocks.

"The empress was a remarkable woman. She had been one of the widows of a monarch, and when his son succeeded to the throne she married him. She had great ambition and great ability. She put down her enemies, and she put herself forward. She took her husband's place in all the imperial consultations and decisions, and very soon set him aside, and for forty years was actual ruler of the empire.

"She was a great woman, this Empress Woo. Very little happened in her dominions that she did not know, and when two wanderers arrived from the far and unknown West, she sent for me and my wife to appear before her at the palace. We were received with much favor, for we could do her no possible harm, and she was very eager for knowledge. My wife was an object of great curiosity to her, as she was so different from the Chinese women.

"But as poor Rina could never acquire a word of the language of the country, the empress soon ceased to take interest in her. As I was always very good at picking up languages, she had me at the palace a great deal, asking all sorts of questions about the Western countries and people. I was also able to tell her much about bygone ages, which information she thought, of course, I had acquired by reading.

"One day the empress asked me about the marriage customs in the West, and wanted to know how many wives a man could have in our country. She seemed to be so much in earnest, as she spoke, that I was frightened. I did not know what to answer. But fortunately one of her generals was announced, and she did not press the question. As I was leaving the palace, one of the officers of the court took me aside, and told me that the empress was thinking of marrying me, and that I had better put on some fine clothes when I came again. This was terrible news, but I was bound to tell my wife, and we sat up all night talking about it. To escape from that region would have been impossible. We were obliged to stay and face the inevitable, whatever it might be. The question which Rina and I had to decide was a very simple one, but terribly difficult for all that. If I should tell the empress that men of my country believed that it was right to have but one wife, Rina would quickly be disposed of; so she had to decide whether she would rather prefer to die so that I might marry the empress, or to preserve her life and lose her undivided possession of a husband."

"I know what I would have done," said Mrs. Crowder, her eyes very bright; "I would have let her kill me. I would never have consented for thee to marry the wretch."

"That would have pleased her," said Mr. Crowder; "for she would have had me all the same, and you would have been out of the way."

"Then I would not have died," said the little Quakeress, almost fiercely; "I would not have done anything to please her. But I don't know. What did thee and thy wife do?"

"We talked and talked and talked," said Mr. Crowder, "and at last I persuaded her to live; that is to say, not to make herself an obstacle to the wishes of the empress. It was a terrible trial, but she consented. The more insignificant she became, I told her, the greater her chances of safety.

"The next day, the empress summoned me, as I was sure she would do.

" 'You did not tell me,' she said, 'how many wives your men have.' 'That all depends upon the will of our sovereign,' I replied; 'in matrimonial affairs we do as we are commanded. When we have no commands from the throne, our circumstances regulate the matter.' "

"Thee did tell a dreadful lie while thee was about it," said Mrs. Crowder, "but I suppose thee had to."

"You are right there," said her husband; "and my answer pleased the empress. 'That is what I like,' she said. 'The monarch should settle all these matters. I hope some day to settle them in this country.' Then, without any hesitation or preface, she announced her intention of marrying me. 'I greatly need,' she said, 'a learned man for an imperial consort. My present husband

"'ASKING ALL SORTS OF QUESTIONS.'"

knows nothing. I never trust him with any affairs of state. But I have never asked you anything to which you did not give me a satisfactory answer.' Now, my dear," said Mr. Crowder, "you see the reward of vanity. If I had pretended to be a fool instead of aspiring to be a philosopher and an historian, I should never have attracted the interest of the queen."

"And did thee marry her?" asked his wife. "I do so pity poor Rina!"

"I'll tell you how it turned out," he continued. "After pressing me a good deal, the empress said: 'I had intended to marry you in a few days, or as soon as the preparations could be made; but I have now postponed that ceremony. I find that military affairs must occupy me for some time, and it would be better for me at present to marry one of my generals. A military man is what the country needs. But I shall want a counselor of your sort very soon, so you must hold yourself ready to marry me whenever I shall notify you.'

"My instincts prompted me to ask her what the imperial general might be apt to think about the increase in her matrimonial forces, but I was wise enough to hold my tongue. When the general should cease to be of use to her, I knew very well that he would not be likely to offer opposition to anything on earth."

"How glad I am," ejaculated Mrs. Crowder, "that thee didn't ask any questions, and that thee consented to everything the wicked creature said!"

"So am I," he replied; "and I was glad to get out of that palace, which I never entered again. From that day I began to grow old as fast as I could. My hair and beard became very long; I ate but little; I stooped more and more each day, and walked with a staff I began to be very forgetful when people asked me questions. About a year afterward the queen saw me. I was in the crowd near the palace, where I had purposely gone that I might be seen. She looked at me, but gave no sign that she recognized me. The next day an officer came to me, and roughly told me that the empress had no use for dotards in her dominions, and that the sooner I went away the better for me. I afterward heard that the execution of two strangers had been ordered, but that a certain superstition in the mind of the empress had prevented this. She had heard, through persons who had met the Nestorians, that people of our country were protected in some strange manner which she did not understand.

"Rina and I could not leave China, for I had now no money; but we went to a distant province, where I lived for more than ten years, passing as a Chinaman."

"And Rina—poor Rina?" asked Mrs. Crowder.

"She soon died," said her husband. "She was in a state of fear nearly all the time. She could not speak the language, and it may be said that she gave up her life in her pursuit of knowledge. In this respect she was as wonderful a woman as was the Empress Woo."

"And a thousand times better," said Mrs. Crowder, earnestly. "And then?"

"Then," said her husband, "I married a Chinese woman."

"What!" exclaimed Mrs. Crowder, her eyes almost round.

"Yes, my dear; it was a great deal safer for me to be married, and to become as nearly as possible like the people by whom I was surrounded."

"But thee didn't have several wives, did thee?" asked Mrs. Crowder.

"Oh, no," he answered; "I was too poor for anything of that kind to be expected of me. When an opportunity came to join a caravan and get away, I took my Chinese wife with me, and eventually

"'AND ROUGHLY TOLD ME.'"

reached Arabia. There we stayed for a long time, for I found it impossible to prosecute my journeying. Eventually, however, we reached the island of Malta, where my wife lived to be over seventy. Travel, hardships, and danger seemed to agree with her. She never spoke any language but her own, and as she was of a quiet disposition, and took no interest in the things she saw, she generally passed as an imbecile. But she was the first Chinese woman who ever visited Europe."

"I guess thee was very sorry thee brought her before thee got through with her. I don't approve of that matrimonial alliance at all," said Mrs. Crowder.

During this and succeeding evenings of narration, it must not be supposed I sat silent, making no remarks upon what I heard; but, in fact, what I said was of hardly any importance, and certainly not worth introducing into this account of Mr. Crowder's experiences. But the effect of his words upon Mrs. Crowder, as shown both by the play of her features and her frequent questions and exclamations, interested me almost as much as the statements of my host. I had previously known her as the gentlest, the sweetest, and the most attractive of my female acquaintances; but now I found her to be a woman of keen intellect and quick appreciation. Her remarks, which were very frequent, and which I shall not always record, were like seasoning and spice to the narrative of Mr. Crowder. Never before had a wife heard such stories from a husband, and there never could have been a woman who would have heard them with such religious faith. Naturally, she showed me a most friendly confidence. The fact that we were both the loyal disciples of one master was a bond between us. He was so much older than either of us, and he regarded us sometimes with what looked so much like parental affection, that it would not have been surprising if persons, not believers as we were, should have entertained the idea that, in course of time, he would pass away, and that we two should be left to comfort each other as well as we might. But I, who had heard my friend speak of the coming years, could not forget the picture he had drawn of two aged and feeble people, looked up to in love and veneration by a fresh and hearty man of fifty-three.

"Thee never seemed to have any trouble in getting married," said Mrs. Crowder. "Did thee ever stay an old bachelor any length of time?"

Crowder laughed. Such questions from his wife amused him very much.

"I was thinking of changing the subject," said he, "and was about to tell you something which had not anything to do with wives and marriages. I thought you might be tired of that sort of thing."

"Not at all," said she, quickly; "that's just what I want to hear."

"Very well," answered he; "I will give you a little instance of one of my failures in love-making.

"It was long before my visit to Empress Woo; in fact, it was about eleven hundred years before Christ, and I was living in Syria, where I was teaching school in the little town of Timnath. I became very much interested in one of the girls of my class. She was a good deal older than any of the others; in fact, she was a young woman. She had a bright mind, and was eager to learn, and I naturally became interested in her; and in the course of time she pleased me so much that I determined to marry her."

"It seems thee was in the habit of marrying thy scholars," said Mrs. Crowder.

"There is nothing very strange in that," he replied; "a schoolmaster usually becomes very well acquainted with some of his scholars, and if a girl pleases him very much it is not surprising that he should prefer to marry her, or, at least, to try to, than to go out among comparative strangers to look for a wife."

"If I had been in thy place," said Mrs. Crowder, reflectively, "sometimes I would have enjoyed a long rest of bachelordom; it would have been a variety."

"Oh, I have had variety of that kind," said he. "For many succeeding decades I have been widower, or bachelor, whichever you choose to call it.

"As I was saying, this girl pleased me very much. She was good-looking, bright, and witty, and her dark, flashing eyes won her a great deal of attention from the young men of the place; but she would not have anything to do with them. They could not boast much in regard to intelligence or education, nor were any of them in very good circumstances; and so, in spite of my years, she seemed to take very kindly to me, and I made up my mind I would marry her the approaching autumn. I had some money, and there was a house with a piece of land for sale near the town. This I planned to buy, and to settle down as an agriculturist. I was tired of school-teaching."

"No wonder," said Mrs. Crowder, "as thee intended to take out of it its principal attraction."

"We were walking, one evening, over the fields, talking of astronomy, in which she took a great interest, when we saw a man approaching who was evidently a stranger. He was a fellow of medium height, but he gave the impression of great size and vigor. As he came nearer, striding over the rough places, and paying no attention to paths, I saw that he was very broad—shouldered, with a heavy body and thick neck. His legs were probably of average size, but they looked somewhat small in comparison with his body and his long arms, which swung by his sides as he walked. He was a young man, bushy-bearded, with bright and observant eyes. As he passed us, he looked very hard at my companion, and, I am sorry to say, she turned her head and gazed steadfastly at him.

" 'That's a fine figure of a man,' she said. 'He looks strong enough for anything.'

"I didn't encourage her admiration. 'He might be made useful on a farm,' I said; 'if his legs were as big as the rest of him, he could draw a plow as well as an ox.'

"She made no answer to this; but her interest in astronomy seemed to decrease, and she soon proposed that we should turn back to the town. On the way we met the stranger again, and this time he stopped and asked us some questions about the country and the neighborhood. All the time we were talking he and my scholar were looking at each other, and each of them seemed entirely satisfied with the survey. The next day the girl was very inattentive at school, and in the afternoon, when I hoped to take a walk with her, I could not find her, and went out by myself. Before long I saw her sitting under a tree, talking to the stranger of yesterday."

"She was a regular flirt," said Mrs. Crowder.

"Apparently she was," replied her husband; "but although I might have excused her, considering how much better suited this stranger was to her, in point of years at least, I was not willing to withdraw and leave her to another, especially as he might be a person entirely unworthy of her.

"I did not disturb them, but I went back to the town and made some inquiries about the stranger. I found that he was a Danite, and lived with his parents in Zorah, and that his name was Samson. I also learned that his family was possessed of considerable means.

"It soon became plain that it would not be easy for me to carry

"'SHE TURNED HER HEAD.'"

out my marriage plans and settle down among my vines and fig-trees. Samson went home, told his parents of his desire to marry this girl, and in the course of time they all came down to Timnath and made regular matrimonial propositions to her parents."

"Was this the great Samson who tore lions apart and threw down temples?" asked Mrs. Crowder, in amazement.

"The very man," was the reply; "and he was the most formidable rival I ever had in that sort of affair. The proper thing for me to do, according to the custom of the times, would have been to take him aside, as soon as I found that he was paying attentions to my sweetheart, and fight him; but the more I looked at him and his peculiar proportions, the more I was convinced that he was not a man with whom I wanted to fight."

"I should think not," said Mrs. Crowder. "How glad I am thee never touched him!"

"The result might not have been disastrous to me," he said; "for although I have always avoided military matters as much as possible, I was probably better versed in the use of a sword than he was. But I did not care to kill him, and from what I heard of him afterward, I am sure that if he had ever got those long arms around me I should have been a mass of broken bones.

"So, taking everything into consideration, I gave up my plan to marry this girl of Timnath; and I was afterward very glad I did so, for she proved a tricky creature, and entered into a conspiracy to deceive her husband, actually weeping before him seven days in order to worm out of him the secret of his strength."

"I suppose thee never met Delilah?" asked Mrs. Crowder.

"Oh, no," he answered; "before Samson was married I left that part of the world, and I did not make the acquaintance of the attractive young person who was so successful in the grand competition of discovering the source of Samson's strength. In fact, it was nearly a hundred years after that before I heard of those great exploits of Samson which have given him such widespread fame."

"I am glad thee never met Delilah," said Mrs. Crowder, reflectively; "for thee, too, was possessed of a great secret, and she might have gained it from thee."

Chapter Four

"I THINK THEE WAS IN GREAT DANGER," continued Mrs. Crowder, "in that Samson business. It makes me shudder to think, even now, of what might have happened to thee."

"There was not much danger," said he; "for all I had to do was to withdraw, and there was an end to the matter. I have often been in greater danger than that. For instance, I was in the army of Xerxes, compelled to enter it simply because I happened to be in Persia. My sympathies were entirely with the Greeks. My age did not protect me at all. Everybody who in any way could be made useful was dragged into that army. It was known that I had a knowledge of engineering and surveying, and I was taken into the army to help build bridges and lay out camps.

"Here it was that I saw the curious method of counting the soldiers which was adopted by the officers of Xerxes's army. As you may have read, ten thousand men were collected on a plain and made to stand close together in a mass nearly circular in shape. Then a strong fence, with a wide gate to the west and another to the east, was built around them, and I was engaged in the constructing and strengthening of this fence. When the fence was finished, the men were ordered to march out of the inclosure, and other soldiers marched in until it was again entirely filled. This process was repeated until the whole army had been in the inclosure. Thus they got rid of the labor of counting—measuring the army instead of enumerating it. But the results were not accurate. I was greatly interested in the matter, and on three occasions I stood at the exit gate as the soldiers were coming out, and counted them, and the number never amounted to ten thousand. One counting showed less than seven thousand,—the men did not pack themselves together as closely as they were packed the first time,—so I am confident that Xerxes's army was not so large as it was reported to be.

"I became so much interested in the operations and constitution of this great horde of soldiers, attendants, animals, vehicles, and ships, that I went about looking at everything and getting all the information possible. In these days I would have been a war correspondent, and I did act somewhat in that capacity; for I told Herodotus a great many of the facts which he put into his history of this great campaign."

"Thee knew Herodotus?" his wife asked.

"Oh, yes; I worked with him a long time, and gave him information which helped him very much in writing his histories; but it would have been of greater advantage to the world if he had adhered more closely to my statements. I told him what I discovered in regard to the enumeration of the army of Xerxes, but he wanted to make that army as big as he could, and he paid little attention to my remonstrances.

"Herodotus was only four years old when Xerxes invaded Greece, and of course all his knowledge concerning that expedition was second-hand, and by the time he began to write his history of the campaign there were very few people living who knew anything personally about it. If he had not been a man so entirely wrapped up in his own work he would have wondered how anyone of my apparent age could give him so much in the way of personal experience; but he seemed to have no suspicions, and, at any rate, asked no questions, and as I had a great desire that this remarkable historical event should be fully recorded, I helped him as much as I could.

"I had been assisting in the construction, of the canal behind Mount Athos, which Xerxes made in order to afford a short cut for his vessels, and as I had frequently climbed into the various portions of the mountain in order to make surveys of the country below, I had obtained a pretty good knowledge of the neighborhood; and when disaster after disaster began to hurl themselves upon this unfortunate multitude of invaders, I took measures for my safety. I did not want to go back to Persia, even if I could go there, which looked very doubtful after the battle of Salamis, and as I had come into the country with the Persians, it might have been unsafe to show myself with the Greeks; so, remembering what I had seen of the wild regions of Mount Athos, I made my way there, with the intention of dwelling in its rocky fastnesses until the country should become safe for the ordinary wayfarer. As there was no opportunity of teaching school on that desolate mountain—"

"And marrying one of thy scholars," interpolated Mrs. Crowder.

"—I became a sort of hermit," he continued; "but I did not spend my time after the usual fashion of the conventional hermit, who lives on water-cresses and reads great books with a skull to keep the pages open. I built myself a rude cabin under a great rock, and lived somewhat after the fashion of the other inhabitants of that wild region, mostly robbers and outlaws. As I had nothing which anyone would want to steal, I was not afraid of them, and I could occasionally be of a little service to them, especially in the way of rude medical attendance, for which they were willing to pay me by giving me now and then some food.

"I had laid in a stock of writing-materials before I went up on the mountain, and I now went to work with great enthusiasm to set down what I knew of the expedition of Xerxes, and here it was that I made the notes which were afterward so very useful to Herodotus.

"When the country became quieter I went down into the plains, looked over the battlefields, and obtained a great deal of information from the villagers and country-people. I stayed here nearly two years, and had a pretty hard time of it; but when I went away I took with me a very valuable collection of notes.

"For many years I made no use of these notes; but being in Halicarnassus, I heard of Herodotus, who was described as a great scholar and traveler, and engaged in writing history. To him I applied without loss of time, and I made a regular engagement, working several hours with him every day. For this he paid me weekly a sum equal to about two dollars and seventy-five cents of our present money; but it was enough to support me, and I was very glad to have the opportunity of sending some of my experiences and observations down into history. It, was at this time that the love of literary work began to arise within me, and in the next three or four centuries after the death of Herodotus I wrote a number of books on various subjects and under various names, and some of these, as I mentioned before, were destroyed with the Alexandrian Library.

"It was in this period that I made the acquaintance of an editor—the first editor, in fact, of whom I know anything at all. I was in Rhodes, and there was a learned man there named Andronicus, who was engaged in editing the works of Aristotle. All the manuscripts and books which that great philosopher left behind him had been given to a friend, or trustee, and had passed from this person into the possession of others, so that for about a hundred years the world knew nothing of them. Then they came into the hands of Andronicus, who undertook to edit them and get them into proper shape for publication. I went to Andronicus, and as soon as he found I was a person qualified for such work, he engaged me as his assistant editor. I held this position for several years, and two or three of the books of Aristotle I transcribed entirely with my own hand, properly shaping sentences and paragraphs, and very often making the necessary divisions. From my experience with Andronicus, I am sure that none of the works of Aristotle were given to the world exactly as he wrote them, for we often found his manuscript copies very rough and disjointed so far as literary construction is concerned, but I will also say that we never interfered with his philosophical theories or his scientific statements and deductions."

"In all that time thee never married?" asked Mrs. Crowder.

Crowder and I could not help laughing. "I did not say so," said he, "but I will say that, with one exception, I do not remember any interesting matrimonial alliances which occurred during the period of my literary labors. I married a young woman of Rhodes, and gave her a very considerable establishment, which I was able to do, for Andronicus paid me much better than Herodotus had done; but she did not prove a very suitable helpmate, and I believe she married me simply because I was in fairly good circumstances. She soon showed that she preferred a young man to an elderly student, the greater part of whose time was occupied with books and manuscripts, and we had not been married a year when she ran away with a young goldsmith, and disappeared from Rhodes, as I discovered, on a vessel bound for Rome. I resigned myself to my loss, and did not even try to obtain news of her. I was too much engrossed in my work to be interested in a runaway wife.

"It was a little more than half a century after this that I was in Rome and sitting on the steps of one of the public buildings in the Forum. I was waiting to meet someone with whom I had business, and while I sat there an old woman stopped in front of me. She was evidently poor, and wretchedly dressed; her scanty hair was gray, and her face was wrinkled and shrunken. I thought, of course, she was a beggar, and was about to give her something, when she clasped her hands in front of her and exclaimed, 'How like! How like!' 'Like whom?' said I. 'What are you talking about?' 'Like your father,' she said, 'like your father! You are so like him, you resemble him so much in form and feature, in the way you sit, in everything, that you must be his son!' 'I have no doubt I am my father's son,' said I, 'and what do you know about him?' 'I married him,' she said. 'For nearly a year I was his wife, and then I foolishly ran away and left him. What became of him I know not, nor how long he lived, but he was a great deal older than I was, and must have passed away many years ago. But thou art his image. He had the same ruddy face, the same short white hair, the same broad shoulders, the same way of crossing his legs as he sat. He must have married soon after I left him. Tell me, whom did he marry? What was thy mother's name?' I gave her the name of my real mother, and she shook her head. 'I never heard of her,' she said. 'Did thy father ever speak of me a wife who ran away from him?' 'Yes; he has spoken of you — that is, if you are Zalia, the daughter of an oil-merchant of Rhodes?'

"'I am that woman,' she exclaimed, 'I am that woman! And did he mourn my loss?'

"'Not much, I think, not much.' Then I became a little nervous, for if this old woman talked to me much longer I was afraid, in spite of the fact that I was an elderly man when she was a girl, that she would become convinced that I could not be the son of the

"'HOW LIKE!'"

man who had once been her husband, but must be that man himself. So I hastily excused myself on the plea of business, and after having given her some money I left her."

"And did thee never see her again?" his wife asked, almost with tears in her eyes. "No, I never saw her again," said Mr. Crowder; "I was careful not to do that but I did not neglect her; I caused good care to be taken of her until she died."

There was a slight pause here, and then Mrs. Crowder said:

"Thee has known a great deal of poverty; in nearly all thy stories thee is a poor man."

"There is good reason for that," said Mr. Crowder; "poor people frequently have more adventures, at least more interesting ones, than those who are in easy circumstances. Possession of money is apt to make life smoother and more commonplace; so, in selecting the most interesting events of my career to tell you, I naturally describe periods of comparative poverty—and there were some periods in which I was in actual want of many of the necessaries of life.

"But you must not suppose that I have always been poor. I have had my periods of wealth, but, as I explained to you before, it was very difficult, on account of the frequent necessity of changing my place of residence, as well as my identity, to carry over my property from one set of conditions to another. However, I have often been able to do this, and at one time I was in comfortable circumstances for nearly two hundred years. But generally, when I found myself obliged to leave a place where I had been living, for fear of suspicion concerning my true age, I had to leave everything behind me.

"I will tell you a story about one of my attempts to provide for the future. It was toward the end of the fifteenth century, about the time that Columbus set out on his first voyage of discovery,—

and you would be surprised, considering the important results of his voyage, to know how little sensation it caused in Europe,—that I devised a scheme by which I thought I might establish for myself a permanent fortune. I was then living in Genoa, and was carrying on the same business in which I am now engaged. I was a broker, a dealer in money and commercial paper. I was prosperous and well able to carry out the plan I had formed. This plan was a simple one. I would purchase jewels, things easily carried about or concealed, and which would be valuable in any country or any age; and with this idea in my mind I spent many years in collecting valuable stones and jewels, confining myself generally to rings, for I wished to make the bulk of my treasures very small when compared with their value.

"About the middle of the sixteenth century I went to Rome, and took my jewels with me. They were then a wonderfully fine collection of gems, some of them of great antiquity and value; for, in gradually gathering them together, the enthusiasm of the collector had possessed me, and I often traveled far to possess myself of a valuable jewel of which I had heard. I remained in Rome as long as I dared do so, and then prepared to set out for Egypt, which I had not visited for a long time, and where I expected to find interesting though depressing changes. I concluded, naturally enough, that it would be dangerous for me to take my treasures with me, and I could conceive of no place where it would be better to leave them than in the Eternal City. Rome was central and comparatively easy of access from any part of the world, and, moreover, was less liable to changes than any other place; so I determined to leave my treasures in Rome, and to put them somewhere where they were not likely to be disturbed by the march of improvement, by the desolations of war and conquest, or to become lost to me by the action of nature. I decided to bury them in the catacombs. With these ancient excavations I was familiar, and I believed that in their dark and mysterious recesses I could conceal my jewels, and that I could find them again when I wanted them.

"I procured a small box made of thick bronze, and in this I put all my rings and gems, and with them I inclosed several sheets of parchment, on which I had written, with the fine ink the monks used in engrossing their manuscripts, a detailed description, and frequently a history, of every one of these valuable objects. Having securely fastened up the box, I concealed it in my clothing and then made my way to the catacombs.

"It was a dark and rainy evening, and as the entrances to the catacombs were not guarded in those days, it was not difficult for me to make my way unseen into their interior. I had brought with me a tinder-box and several rushlights, and as soon as I felt secure from observation from the outside I struck a light and began my operations. Then, according to a plan I had previously made, I slowly walked along the solemn passageway which I had entered.

"My plan of procedure was a very simple one, and I had purposely made it so in order that it might be more easily remembered. I was well acquainted with the position of the opening by which I had entered. For several days I had studied carefully its relation to other points in the surrounding country. Starting from this opening, my plan was to proceed inward through the long corridor until I came to a transverse passage; to pass this until I reached another; to pass this also, and to go on until I came to a third; then I would turn to my left and proceed until I had passed two other transverse passages and reached a third; then I would again turn to my left and count the open tombs on my left hand. When I reached the third tomb I would stop. Thus there would be a series of three threes, and it was scarcely possible that I could forget that.

"At this period a great many of the tombs were open, having been despoiled even of the few bones they contained. The opening at which I stopped was quite a large one, and when I put my light inside I found it was entirely empty.

"Lighting another rush-candle, I stuck it in the bottom of the tomb, which was about four feet above the floor of the passage, and drawing my large dagger, I proceeded to dig a hole in the left-hand corner nearest the front. The earth was dry and free from stones, and I soon made a hole two feet deep, at the bottom of which I placed my box. Then I covered it up, pressing the earth firmly down into the hole. When this was entirely filled, I smoothed away the rest of the earth I had taken out, and after I finished my work, the floor of the tomb did not look as if it had been disturbed. Then I went away, reached the passage three tombs from me, turned to the right, went on until I reached the third transverse passage, then went on until I came to the entrance. It was raining heavily, but I was glad to get out into the storm."

"Now, please hurry on," said Mrs. Crowder. "When did thee get them again?"

"A great many things happened in Egypt," said Mr. Crowder, "some pleasant and some unpleasant, and they kept me there a long time. After that I went to Constantinople, and subsequently resided in Greece and in Venice. I lived very comfortably during the greater part of this period, and therefore there was no particular reason why I should go after my jewels. So it happened that, for one cause or another, I did not go back to Rome until early in the nineteenth century, and I need not assure you that almost the first place I visited was the catacombs.

"'I PROCEEDED TO DIG A HOLE.'"

"After three hundred years of absence I found the entrance, but if I had not so well noted its position in relation to certain ruins and natural objects I should not have recognized it. It was not now a wide opening through which a man might walk; it was a little hole scarcely big enough for a fox to crawl through; in fact, I do not believe there would have been any opening there at all if it had not been for the small animals living in the catacombs, which had maintained this opening for the purpose of going in and out. It was broad daylight when I found this entrance. Of course I did not attempt to do anything then, but in the night, when there was no moon, I came with a spade. I enlarged the hole, crawled through, and after a time found myself in a passageway, which was unobstructed."

"Now, hurry on," said Mrs. Crowder.

"I brought no rushlights with me this time," said Mr. Crowder. "I had a good lantern, and I walked steadily on until I came to the third transverse passage; I turned to the left, counted three more passages; I turned to the left, I walked on slowly, I examined the left-hand wall, and apparently there were no open tombs. This startled me, but I soon found that I had been mistaken. I saw some tombs which were not open, but which had been opened and were now nearly filled with the dust of ages. I stopped before the first of these; then I went on and clearly made out the position of another; then I came to the third: that was really open, although the aperture was much smaller than it had been. It did not look as I remembered it, but without hesitation I took a trowel which I had brought with me, and began to dig in the nearest left-hand corner.

"I dug and I dug until I had gone down more than two feet; then I dug on and on until, standing in the passage as I was, I could not reach down any deeper into the hole I had made. So I crawled into the tomb, crouched down on my breast, and dug down and down as far as I could reach.

"Then," said Mr. Crowder, looking at us as he spoke, "I found the box."

A great sigh of relief came from Mrs. Crowder.

"I was so afraid," said she—"I was so afraid it had sunk out of reach."

"No," said he; "its weight had probably made it settle down, and then the dust of ages, as I remarked before, had accumulated over it. That sort of thing is going on in Rome all the time. But I found my box, and, after hours and hours of wandering, I got out of the catacombs."

"How was that?" we both asked.

"I was so excited at the recovery of my treasures after the lapse of three centuries that when I turned into the first passage I forgot to count those which crossed it, and my mind became so thoroughly mixed up in regard to this labyrinth that I don't know when I would have found my way out if I had not heard a little animal—I don't know what it was—scurrying away in front of me. I followed it, and eventually saw a little speck of light. That proved to be the hole through which I had come in."

"What *did* thee do with the jewels?" asked Mrs. Crowder.

Her husband looked at his watch, and then held it with the face toward her. She gave a cry of surprise, and we all went upstairs to bed.

Chapter Five

"Now, my dear," said Mrs. Crowder, the moment we had finished dinner on the next evening, "I want thee to tell us immediately what thee did with the jewels. I have been thinking about that all day; and I believe, if I had been with thee, I could have given thee some good advice, so that the money thee received for these treasures would have lasted thee a long time."

"I have thought on that subject many times," said Mr. Crowder, "not only in regard to this case, but others, and have formed hundreds of plans for carrying my possessions into another set of social conditions; but the fact of being obliged to change my identity always made it impossible for me to avail myself of the advantages of commercial paper, legal deeds, and all titles to property."

"Thee might have put thy wealth into solid gold—great bars and lumps. Those would be available in any country and in any age, and they wouldn't have had anything to do with thy identity," said his wife.

"It was always difficult for me to carry about or even conceal such golden treasures, but I have sometimes done it. However, as you are in such a hurry to hear about the jewels, I will let all other subjects drop. When I reached my lodgings in Rome, I opened the box, and found everything perfect; the writing on the sheets of parchment was still black and perfectly legible, and the jewels looked just as they did when I put them into the box."

"I cannot imagine," interrupted Mrs. Crowder, "how thee remembered what they looked like after the lapse of three hundred years."

Mr. Crowder smiled. "You forget," he said, "that since I first reached the age of fifty-three there has been no radical change in me, physical or mental. My memory is just as good now as it was when I reached my fifty-third birthday, in the days of Abraham. It is impossible for me to forget anything of importance, and I remembered perfectly the appearance of those gems. But my knowledge of such things had been greatly improved by time and experience, and after I had spent an hour or two looking over my treasures, I felt sure that they were far more valuable than they were when they came into my possession. In fact, it was a remarkable collection of precious stones, considering it in regard to its historic as well as its intrinsic value.

"I shall not attempt to describe my various plans for disposing of my treasures; but I soon found that it would not be wise for me to try to sell them in Rome. I had picked out one of the least valuable engraved stones, and had taken it to a lapidary, who readily bought it at his own valuation, and paid me with great promptness; but after he had secured it he asked me so many questions about it, particularly how I had come into possession of it, that I was very sure that he had made a wonderful bargain, and was also convinced that it would not do for me to take any more of my gems to him. Those Roman experts knew too much about antique jewels.

"I went to Naples, where I had a similar experience. Then I found it would be well for me, if I did not wish to be arrested as a thief who had robbed a museum, to endeavor to sell my collection as a whole in some other country. As a professional dealer in gems from a foreign land I would be less liable to suspicion than if I endeavored to peddle my jewels one at a time. So I determined to go to Madrid and try to sell my collection there.

"When I reached Spain I found the country in a great turmoil. This was in 1808, when Napoleon was on the point of invading Spain; but as politicians, statesmen, and military men were not in the habit of buying ancient gems, I still hoped that I might be able to transact the business which had brought me to the country. My collection would be as valuable to a museum then as at any time; for it was not supposed that the French were coming into the country to ravage and destroy the great institutions of learning and art. I made acquaintances in Madrid, and before long I had an opportunity of exhibiting my collection to a well-known dealer and connoisseur, who was well acquainted with the officers of the Royal Museum. I thought it would be well to sell them through his agency, even though I paid a high commission.

"If I should say that this man was astounded as well as delighted when he saw my collection, I should be using very feeble expressions; for, carried away by his enthusiasm, he did not hesitate to say to me that it was the most valuable collection he had ever seen. Even if the stones had been worthless in themselves, their historic value was very great. Of course, he wanted to know where I had obtained these treasures, and I informed him truthfully that I had traveled far and wide in order to gather them together. I told him the history of many of them, but entirely omitted mentioning anything which would give a clue to the times and periods when I had come into possession of them.

"This dealer undertook the sale of my jewels. We arranged them in a handsome box lined with velvet and divided into compartments, and I made a catalogue of them, copied from my ancient parchments—which would have ruined me had I inadvertently allowed them to be seen. He put himself into communication with the officers of the museum, and I left the matter entirely in his hands.

"In less than a week I became aware that I was an object of suspicion. I called on the dealer, but he was not to be seen. I found that I was shadowed by officers of the law. I wrote to the dealer, but received no answer. One evening, when I returned to my lodgings, I found that they had been thoroughly searched. I became alarmed, and the conviction forced itself upon me that the sooner I should escape from Madrid, the better for me."

"What!" exclaimed Mrs. Crowder, "and leave thy jewels behind? Thee certainly did not do that!"

"Ah, my dear," replied her husband, "you do not comprehend the situation. It was very plain that the authorities of the museum did not believe that a private individual, a stranger, was likely to be the legitimate owner of these treasures. Had my case been an ordinary one I should have courted investigation; but how could I prove that I had been an honest man three hundred years before? A legal examination, not so much on account of the jewels, but because of the necessary assertion of my age, would have been a terrible ordeal.

"I hurried to the dealer's shop, but found it closed. Inquiring of a woman on a neighboring door-step, I was informed that the dealer had been arrested. I asked no more. I did not return to my lodgings, and that night I left Madrid."

I could not repress an exclamation of distress, and Mrs. Crowder cried: "Did thee really go away and leave thy jewels? Such a thing is too dreadful to think of. But perhaps thee got them again?"

"No," said Mr. Crowder; "I never saw them again, nor ever

heard of them. But now that it is impossible for anyone to be living who might recognize me, I hope to go to Madrid and see those gems. I have no doubt that they are in the museum."

"And I," exclaimed Mrs. Crowder—"I shall go with thee; I shall see them."

"Indeed you shall," said her husband, taking her affectionately by the hand. And then he turned to me. "You may think," said he, "that I was too timid, that I was too ready to run away from danger; but it is hard for anyone but myself readily to appreciate my horror of a sentence to imprisonment or convict labor for life."

"Oh, horrible!" said his wife, with tears in her eyes. "Then thee would have despaired indeed."

"No," said he; "I should not even have had that consolation. Despair is a welcome to death. I can tell you, that a man who cannot die cannot truly despair. But do not let us talk upon such a melancholy subject."

"No, no," cried Mrs. Crowder; "I am glad thee left those wretched jewels behind thee. And thee got away safely?"

"Oh, yes; I had some money left. I traveled by night and concealed myself by day, and so got out of Spain. Soon after I crossed the Pyrenees I found myself penniless, and was obliged to work my way."

"Poverty again!" exclaimed Mrs. Crowder. "It is dreadful to hear so much of it. If thee could only have carried away with thee one of thy diamonds, thee might have cracked it up into little pieces, and thee might have sold these, one at a time, without suspicion."

"I never thought of being a vender of broken diamonds, and there is nothing suspicious about honest labor. The object of my present endeavors was to reach England, and I journeyed northward. It was nearly a month after I had entered France that I was at a little village on the Garonne, repairing a stone wall which divided a field from the road, and I assure you I was very glad to get this job.

"It was here that I heard of the near approach of Napoleon's army on its march into Spain; that the news was true was quickly proved, for very soon after I had begun my work on the wall the country to the north seemed to be filled with cavalry, infantry, artillery, baggage-wagons, and everything that pertained to an army. About noon there was a general halt, and in the field the wall of which I was repairing a body of officers made a temporary encampment.

"I paid as little apparent attention as possible to what was going on around me, but proceeded steadily with my work, although I assure you I had my eyes wide open all the time. I was thinking of stopping work in order to eat my dinner, which I had with me, when a party of officers approached me on their way to a little hill in the field. One of them stopped and spoke to me, and as he did so the others halted and stood together a little way off. The moment I looked at the person who addressed me I knew him. It was Napoleon Bonaparte."

"Then thee has seen the great Napoleon," almost whispered Mrs. Crowder.

"And very much disappointed I was when I beheld him," remarked her husband. "I had seen portraits of him, I had read and heard of his great achievements, and I had pictured to myself a hero. Perhaps my experience should have taught me that heroes seldom look like heroes, but for all that I had had my ideal, and in appearance this man fell below it. His face was of an olive color which was unequally distributed over his features; he was inclined to be pudgy, and his clothes did not appear to fit him; but for all that he had the air of a man who with piercing eyes saw his way before him and did not flinch from taking it, however rough it might be. 'You seem an old man for such work,' said he, 'but if you are strong enough to lift those stones why are you not in the army?' As he spoke I noticed that he had not the intonation of a true Frenchman. He had the accent of the foreigner that he was.

"'Sire,' said I, 'I am too old for the army, but in spite of my age I must earn my bread.' I may state here that my hair and beard had been growing since I left Madrid. For a moment the emperor regarded me in silence. 'Are you a Frenchman?' said he. 'You speak too well for a stone-mason, and, moreover, your speech is that of a foreigner who has studied French.' It was odd that each of us should have remarked the accent of the other, but I was not amused at this; I was becoming very nervous. 'Sire,' said I, 'I come from Italy.' 'Were you born there?' asked he. My nervousness increased. This man was too keen a questioner. 'Sire,' I replied, 'I was born in the country south east of Rome.' This was true enough, but it was a long way southeast. 'Do you speak Spanish?' he abruptly asked.

"At this question my blood ran cold. I had had enough of speaking Spanish. I was trying to get away from Spain and everything that belonged to that country; but I thought it safest to speak the truth, and I answered that I understood the language. The emperor now beckoned to one of his officers, and ordered him to talk with me in Spanish. I had been in Spain in the early part of the preceding century, and I had there learned to speak the pure Castilian tongue, so that when the officer talked with me I could see that he was surprised, and presently he told the emperor that he had never heard anyone who spoke such excellent Spanish. The emperor fixed his eyes upon me. 'You must have traveled a great deal,' he said. 'You should not be wasting your time with stones and mortar.' Then, turning to the officer who had spoken to me, he said, 'He understands Spanish so well that we may make him useful.' He was about to address me again, but was interrupted by the arrival of an orderly with a despatch. This he read hastily, and walked toward the officers who were waiting for him; but before he left me he ordered me to report myself at his tent, which was not far off in the field. He then walked away, evidently discussing the despatch, which he still held open in his hand.

"Now I was again plunged into the deepest apprehension and fear. I did not want to go back to Spain, not knowing what might happen to me there. Every evil thing was possible. I might be recognized, and the emperor might not care to shield anyone claimed by the law as an escaped thief. In an instant I saw all sorts of dreadful possibilities. I determined to take no chances. The moment the emperor's back was turned upon me I got over the broken part of the wall and, interfered with by no one, passed quietly along the road to the house of the man who had employed me to do his mason-work, and seeing no one there, — for every window and door was tightly closed,—I walked into the yard and went to the well, which was concealed from the road by some shrubbery. I looked quickly about, and perceiving that I was not in sight of anyone, I got into the well and went down to the bottom, assisting my descent by the well-rope. The water was about five feet deep, and when I first entered it, it chilled me; but nothing could chill me so much as the thought that I might be taken back into Spain, no matter by whom or for what. I must admit that I was doing then, and often had done, that which seemed very much like cowardice; but people who can die cannot understand the fear which may come upon a person who has not that refuge from misfortune.

"For the rest of the day I remained in the well, and when people came to draw water — and this happened many times in the

"'WHY ARE YOU NOT IN THE ARMY?'"

course of the afternoon — I crouched down as much as I could; but at such times I would have been concealed by the descending bucket, even if anyone had chosen to look down the well. This bucket was a heavy one with iron hoops, and I had a great deal of trouble sometimes to shield my head from it."

"I should think thee would have taken thy death of cold," said Mrs. Crowder, "staying in that cold well the whole afternoon."

"No," said her husband, with a smile; "I was not afraid of that. If I should have taken cold I knew it would not be fatal, and although the water chilled me at first, I became used to it. An hour or two after nightfall I clambered up the well-rope, and it was not an easy thing, for although not stout, I am a heavy man, — and I got away over the fields with all the rapidity possible. I did not look back to see if the army were still on the road, nor did I ever know whether I had been searched for or had been forgotten.

"I shall not describe the rest of my journey. There is nothing remarkable about it except that it was beset with many hardships. I made my way into Switzerland and so on down the Rhine, and it was nearly seven months after I left Madrid before I reached England.

"I remained many years in Great Britain, living here and there, and was greatly interested in the changes and improvements I saw around me. You can easily understand this when I tell you it was in 1512, twenty years after the discovery of America, that I had last been in England. I do not believe that in any other part of the world the changes in three hundred years could have been more marked and impressive.

"I had never visited Ireland, and as I had a great desire to see that country. I made my way there as soon as possible, and after visiting the most noted spots of the island I settled down to work as a gardener."

"Always poor," ejaculated Mrs. Crowder, with a sigh.

"No, not always," answered her husband. "But wandering sightseers cannot be expected to make much money. At this time I was very glad indeed to cease from roving and enjoy the comforts of a home, even though it were a humble one. The family with whom I took service was that of Maria Edgeworth, who lived with her father in Edgeworthstown."

"What!" cried Mrs. Crowder, "'Lazy Lawrence,' 'Simple Susan,' and all the rest of them? Was it that Miss Edgeworth?"

"Certainly," said he; "there never was but one Maria Edgeworth, and I don't think there ever will be another. I soon became very well acquainted with Miss Edgeworth. Her father was a studious man and a magistrate. He paid very little attention to the house and garden, the latter of which was almost entirely under the charge of his daughter Maria. She used to come out among the flower-beds and talk to me, and as my varied experience enabled me to tell her a great deal about fruits, flowers, and vegetables, she became more and more interested in what I had to tell her. She was a plain, sensible woman, anxious for information, and she lived in a very quiet neighborhood where she did not often have opportunities of meeting persons of intelligence and information. But when she found out that I could tell her so many things, not only about plants but about the countries where I had known them, she would sometimes spend an hour or two with me, taking notes of what I said.

"During the time that I was her gardener she wrote the story of 'The Little Merchants,' and as she did not know very much about Italy and Naples, I gave her most of the points for that highly moral story. She told me, in fact, that she did not believe she could have written it had it not been for my assistance. She thought well to begin the story by giving some explanatory

'Extracts from a Traveler's Journal' relative to Italian customs, but afterward she depended entirely on me for all points concerning distinctive national characteristics and the general Italian atmosphere. As she became aware that I was an educated man and had traveled in many countries, she was curious about my antecedents, but of course my remarks in that direction were very guarded.

"One day, as she was standing looking at me as I was pruning a rose-bush, she made a remark which startled me. I perfectly remember her words. 'It seems to me,' she said, 'that one who is so constantly engaged in observing and encouraging the growth and development of plants should himself grow and develop. Roses of one year are generally better than those of the year before. Then why is not the gardener better?' To these words she immediately added, being a woman of kind impulses, 'But in the case of a good gardener, such as you are, I've no doubt he does grow better, year by year.' "

"What was there so startling in that little speech?" asked Mrs. Crowder. "I don't think she could have said anything less."

"I will tell you why I was startled," said her husband. "Almost those very words—mark me, almost those very words—had been said to me when I was working in the wonderful gardens of Nebuchadnezzar, and he was standing by me watching me prune a rose-bush. That Maria Edgeworth and the great Nebuchadnezzar should have said the same thing to me was enough to startle me."

To this astounding statement Mrs. Crowder and I listened with wide-open eyes. "Yes," said Mr. Crowder; "you may think it amazing that a very ordinary remark should connect 'The Parents' Assistant' with the city of Babylon, but so it was. In the course of my life I have noticed coincidences quite as strange.

"I spent many years in the city of Babylon, but the wonderful Hanging Gardens interested me more than anything else the great city contained. At the time of which I have just spoken I was one of Nebuchadnezzar's gardeners, but not in the humble position which I afterward filled in Ireland. I had under my orders fifteen slaves, and my principal duty was to direct the labors of these poor men. These charming gardens, resting upon arches high above the surface of the ground, watered by means of pipes from the river Euphrates, and filled with the choicest flowers, shrubs, and plants known to the civilization of the time, were a ceaseless source of delight to me. Often, when I had finished the daily work assigned to me and my men, I would wander over other parts of the garden and enjoy its rare beauties.

"I frequently met Nebuchadnezzar, who for the time enjoyed his gardens almost as much as I did. When relieved from the cares of state and his ambitious plans, and while walking in the winding paths among sparkling fountains and the fragrant flowerbeds, he seemed like a very ordinary man, quiet and reflective, with very good ideas concerning nature and architecture. The latter I learned from his frequent remarks to me. I suppose it was because I appeared to be so much older and more experienced than most of those who composed his little army of gardeners that he often addressed me, asking questions and making suggestions; and it was one afternoon, standing by me as I was at work in a rose-bed, that he said the words which were spoken to me about twenty-four centuries afterward by Maria Edgeworth. Now, wasn't that enough to startle a man?"

"Startle!" exclaimed Mrs. Crowder, "I should have screamed. I should have thought that someone had come from the dead to speak to me. But I suppose there was nothing about Edgeworth which reminded thee of Nebuchadnezzar, King of Babylon."

NEBUCHADNEZZAR AND THE GARDENER.

"Yes, there was," replied her husband "there was the same meditative expression of the eyes; the same reflective mood as each one began to speak, as if he and she were merely thinking aloud; the same quick, kind reference to me, as if the speaker feared that my feelings might have been hurt by a presumption that I myself had not developed and improved.

"I had good reason to remember those words of Nebuchadnezzar, for they were the last I ever heard him speak. A few days afterward I was informed by the chief gardener that the king was about to make a journey across the mountains into Media, and that he intended to establish there what would now be called an experimental garden of horticulture, which was to be devoted to growing and improving certain ornamental trees which did not flourish in the Hanging Gardens of Babylon. His expedition was not to be undertaken entirely for this purpose, but he was a man who did a great many things at once, and the establishment of these experimental grounds was only one of the objects of his journey.

"The chief gardener then went on to say that the king had spoken to him about me and had said that he would take me with him and perhaps put me in charge of the new gardens.

"This mark of royal favor did not please me at all. I had hoped that I might ultimately become the chief of the Babylonian gardens, and this would have suited me admirably. It was a position of profit and some honor, and when I thought that I had lived long enough in that part of the world it would have been easy for me to make a journey into the surrounding country on some errand connected with the business of the gardens, and then quietly to disappear. But if I were to be taken into Media it might not be easy for me to get away. Therefore, I did not wait to see Nebuchadnezzar again and to receive embarrassing royal commands, but I went to my home that night, and returned no more to the wonderful Hanging Gardens of Babylon."

"I think thee was a great deal better off in the gardens of Maria Edgeworth," said Mrs. Crowder, "for there thee could come and go as thee pleased, and it almost makes my flesh creep when I think of thee living in company with the bloody tyrants of the past. And always in poverty and suffering, as if thee had been one of the common people, and not the superior of every man around thee! I don't want to hear anything more about the wicked Nebuchadnezzar. How long did thee stay with Maria Edgeworth?"

"About four years," he replied; "and I might have remained much longer, for in that quiet life the advance of one's years was not likely to be noticed. I am sure Miss Edgeworth looked no older to me when I left her than when I first saw her. But she was obliged to go into England to nurse her sick stepmother, and after her departure the place had no attractions for me, and I left Ireland."

"I wonder," said Mrs. Crowder, a little maliciously, "that thee did not marry her."

Her husband laughed.

"Englishwomen of her rank in society do not marry their gardeners, and, besides, in any case, she would not have suited me for a wife. For one reason, she was too homely."

"Oh," exclaimed Mrs. Crowder, and she might have said more, but her husband did not give her a chance.

"I know I have talked a great deal about my days of poverty and misery, and now I will tell you something different. For a time I was the ruler of all the Russias."

"Ruler!" exclaimed Mrs. Crowder and I, almost in the same breath.

"Yes," said he, "absolute ruler. And this was the way of it:

"I was in Russia in the latter part of the seventeenth century, at a time when there was great excitement in royal and political circles. The young czar Feodor had recently died, and he had named as his successor his half-brother Peter, a boy ten years of age, who afterward became Peter the Great. The late czar's young brother Ivan should have succeeded him, but he was almost an idiot. In this complicated state of things, the half-sister of Peter, the Princess Sophia, a young woman of wonderful ambition and really great abilities, rose to the occasion. She fomented a revolution; there was fighting, with all sorts of cruelties and horrors, and when affairs had quieted down she was princess regent, while the two boys, Ivan and Peter, were waiting to see what would happen next.

"She was really a woman admirably adapted to her position. She was well educated, wrote poetry, and knew how to play her part in public affairs. She presided in the councils, and her authority was without control; but she was just as bloody-minded and cruel as anybody else in Russia.

"Now, it so happened when the Princess Sophia was at the height of her power, that I was her secretary. For five or six years I had been a teacher of languages in Moscow, and at one time I had given lessons to the princess. In this way she had become well acquainted with me, and having frequently called upon me for information of one sort or another, she concluded to make me her secretary. Thus I was established at the court of Russia. I had charge of all Sophia's public papers, and I often had a good deal to do with her private correspondence, but she signed and sealed all papers of importance.

"The Prince Galitzin, who had been her father's minister and was now Sophia's main supporter in all her autocratic designs and actions, found himself obliged to leave Moscow to attend to his private affairs on his great estates, and to be absent for more than a month; and after his departure the princess depended on me more than ever. Like many women in high positions, it was absolutely necessary for her to have a man on whom she could lean with one hand while she directed her affairs with the other."

"I do not think that is always necessary," said Mrs. Crowder, "at least, in these days."

"Perhaps not," said her husband, with a smile, "but it was then. But I must get on with my story. One morning soon after Galitzin's departure, the horses attached to the royal sledge ran away just outside of Moscow. The princess was thrown out upon the hard ground, and badly dislocated her right wrist. By the time she had been taken back to the palace her arm and hand were dreadfully swollen, and it was difficult for her surgeons to do anything for her.

"I was called into the princess's room just after the three surgeons had been sent to prison. I found her in great trouble, mental as well as physical, and her principal anxiety was that she was afraid it would be a long time before she would be able to use her hand and sign and seal the royal acts and decrees. She had a certain superstition about this which greatly agitated her. If she could not sign and seal, she did not believe she would be able to rule. Anyone who understood the nature of the political factions in Russia well knew that an uprising among the nobles might occur upon any pretext, and no pretext could be so powerful as the suspicion of incompetency in the sovereign. The seat of a ruler who did not rule was extremely uncertain.

"At that moment a paper of no great importance, which had been sent in to her before she went out in her sledge that morning, was lying on the table near her couch, and she was greatly worried because she could not sign it. I assured her she need not trouble herself about it, for I could attend to it. I had often affixed her initials and seal to unimportant papers.

"The princess did not object to my proposition, but this was not enough for her. She had a deep mind, and she quickly concocted a scheme by which her public business should be attended to, while at the same time it should not be known that she did not attend to it. She caused it to be given out that it was her ankle which had been injured, and not her wrist. She sent for another surgeon, and had him locked up in the palace when he was not attending to her, so that he should tell no tales. Her ladies were informed that it would be very well for them to keep silent, and they understood her. Then she arranged with me that all public business should be brought to her; that I should sign and seal in her place, and should be her agent of communication with the court.

"When this plan had been settled upon, the princess regained something of her usual good spirits. 'As I never sign my name with my toes,' she said to me, 'there is no reason why a sprained ankle should interfere with my royal functions, and, for the present, you can be my right hand.'

"This was a very fine plan, but it did not work as she expected it would. Her wrist became more and more painful, and fever set in, and on the second day, when I called upon her, I found she was in no condition to attend to business. She was irritable and drowsy. 'Don't annoy me with that paper,' she said. 'If the wool-dealers ought to have their taxes increased, increase them. You should not bring these trifles to me; but'—and now she regained for a moment her old acuteness—'remember this: don't let my administration stop.'

"I understood her very well, and when I left her I saw my course plain before me. It was absolutely necessary that the exercise of royal functions by the Princess Sophia should appear to go on in its usual way; any stoppage would be a signal for a revolution. In order that this plan should be carried out, I must act for the princess regent; I must do what I thought right, and it must be done in her name, exactly as if she had ordered it. I assumed the responsibilities without hesitation. While it was supposed I was merely the private secretary of the princess, acting as her agent and mouthpiece, I was in fact the ruler of all the Russias."

Mrs. Crowder opened her mouth as if she would gasp for breath, but she did not say anything.

"You can scarcely imagine, my dear," said he, "the delight with which I assumed the powers so suddenly thrust upon me. I set myself to work without delay, and, as I knew all about the wool-dealers' business, I issued a royal decree decreasing their taxes. Poor creatures! they were suffering enough already."

"Good for thee!" exclaimed Mrs. Crowder.

"I cannot tell you of all the reforms I devised, or even those which I carried out. I knew that the fever of the princess, aggravated by the inflammation of her dislocated wrist, would continue for some time, and I bent all my energies to the work of doing as much good as I could in the vast empire under my control while I had the opportunity. And it was a great opportunity, indeed! I did not want to do anything so radical as to arouse the opposition of the court, and therefore I directed my principal efforts to the amelioration of the condition of the people in the provinces. It would be a long time before word could get back to the capital of what I had done in those distant regions. By night and by day my couriers were galloping in every direction, carrying good news to the peasants of Russia. It was remarked by some of the councilors, when they spoke of the municipal reforms I instituted, that the princess seemed to be in a very humane state of mind; but none of them cared to interfere with what they supposed to be the sick-bed workings of her conscience. So I ruled with a high hand, astonishing the provincial officials, and causing thousands of downtrodden subjects to begin to believe that perhaps they were really human beings, with some claim on royal justice and kindness.

"I fairly reveled in my imperial power, but I never forgot to be prudent. I lessened the duties and slightly increased the pay of the military regiments stationed in and about Moscow, and thus the Princess Sophia became very popular with the army, and I felt safe. I went in to see the princess every day, and several times when she was in her right mind she asked me if everything was going on well, and once when I assured her that all was progressing quietly and satisfactorily, she actually thanked me. This was actually a good deal for a Russian princess. If she had known how the people were thanking her, I do not know what would have happened.

"For twenty-one days I reigned over Russia. If I had been able to do it, I should have made each day a year; I felt that I was in my proper place."

"And thee was right," said Mrs. Crowder, her eyes sparkling. "I believe that at that time thee was the only monarch in the world who was worthy to reign." And with a loyal pride, as if he had just stepped from a throne, she put her hand upon his arm.

"Yes," said Mr. Crowder, "I honestly believe that I was a good monarch, and I will admit that in those days such personages were extremely scarce. So my imperial sway proceeded with no obstruction—until I was informed that Prince Galitzin was hastening to Moscow, on his return from his estates, and was then within three days' journey of the capital. Now I prepared to lay down the tremendous power which I had wielded with such immense satisfaction to myself, and with such benefit, I do not hesitate to say, to the people of Russia. The effects of my rule are still to be perceived in some of the provinces of Russia, and decrees I made more than two hundred years ago are in force in many villages along the eastern side of the Volga.

"The day before Prince Galitzin was expected, I visited Sophia for the last time. She was a great deal better, and much pleased by the expected arrival of her minister. She even gave me some commands, but when I left her I did not execute them. I would not have my reign sullied by any of her mandates. That afternoon, in a royal sledge, with the royal permission, given by myself, to travel where and how I pleased, I left Moscow. Frequent relays of horses carried me rapidly beyond danger of pursuit, and so, in course of time, I passed the boundaries of the empire of Russia, over which for three weeks I had ruled, an absolute autocrat."

"Does thee know," said Mrs. Crowder, "that two or three times I expected thee to say that thee married Sophia?"

Mr. Crowder laughed. "That is truly a wild notion," said he.

"I don't think it is wild at all," she replied. "In the course of thy life thee has married a great many plain persons. In some ways that princess would have suited thee as a wife, and if thee had really married her and had become her royal consort, like Prince Albert, thee might have made a great change in her. But, after all, it would have been a pity to interfere with the reign of Peter the Great."

Chapter Six

"AND WHAT DID THEE do after thee got out of Russia?"asked Mrs. Crowder, the next evening.

Her husband shook his head. "No, no, my dear; we cannot go on with my autobiography in that fashion. If I should take up my life step by step, there would not be time enough—" There he stopped, but I am sure we both understood his meaning. There would be plenty of time for him!

"Often and often," said Mr. Crowder, after a few minutes' silence, "have I determined to adopt some particular profession, and continue its practice wherever I might find myself; but in this I did not succeed very well. Frequently I was a teacher, but not for many consecutive years. Something or other was sure to happen to turn my energies into other channels."

"Such as falling in love with thy scholars," said his wife.

"You have a good memory," he replied. "That sometimes happened; but there were other reasons which turned me away from the paths of the pedagogue. With my widely extended opportunities, I naturally came to know a good deal of medicine and surgery. On many occasions, I had been a doctor in spite of myself, and as far back as the days of the patriarchs I was called upon to render aid to sick and ailing people.

"In the days when I lived in a cave and gained a reputation as a wise and holy hermit, more people came to me to get relief from bodily ailments than to ask for spiritual counsel. You will remember that I told you that I was visited at that time by Moses and Joshua. Moses came, I truly believe, on account of his desire to become acquainted with the prophet El Khoudr, of whom he had heard so much; but Joshua wanted to see me for an entirely different reason. The two remained with me for about an hour, and although Moses had no belief in me as a prophet, he asked me a great many questions, and I am sure that I proved to him that I was a man of a great deal of information. He had a keen mind, with a quick perception of the motives of others, and in every way was well adapted to be a leader of men.

"When Moses had gone away to a tent about a mile distant, where he intended to spend the night, Joshua remained, and as soon as his uncle was out of sight, he told me why he wished to see me."

"His uncle!" exclaimed Mrs. Crowder.

"Certainly," said her husband; "Joshua was the son of Nun and of Miriam, and Miriam was the sister of Moses and Aaron. What he now wanted from me was medical advice. For some time he had been afflicted with rheumatism in his left leg, which came upon him after exposure to the damp and cold.

"Now, this was a very important thing to Joshua. He was a great favorite with Moses, who intended him, as we all know, to be his successor as leader of the people and of the army. Joshua was essentially a soldier; he was quiet, brave, and a good disciplinarian; in fact, he had all the qualities needed for the position he expected to fill; but he was not young, and if he should become subject to frequent attacks of rheumatism, it is not likely that Moses, who had very rigid ideas of his duties to his people, would be willing to place at their head a man who might at any time be incapacitated from taking his proper place on the field of battle. So Joshua had never mentioned his ailment to his uncle, hoping that he might be relieved of it, and having heard that I was skilled in such matters, now wished my advice.

"I soon found that his ailment was a very ordinary one, which might easily be kept under control, if not cured, and I proceeded at once to apply remedies. I will just mention that in those days remedies were generally heroic, and I think you will agree with me when I tell you how I treated Joshua. I first rubbed his aching muscles with fine sand, keeping up a friction until his skin was in a beautiful glow. Then I brought out from the back part of my cave, where I was keeping my medicines, a jar containing a liniment which I had made for such purposes. It was composed of oil, in which had been steeped the bruised fruit or pods of a plant very much resembling the Tabasco pepper-plant."

"Whoop!" I exclaimed involuntarily.

"Yes," said Mr. Crowder, "and Joshua whooped too. But it was a grand liniment, especially when applied upon skin already excited by rubbing with sand. He jumped at first, but he was a soldier, and he bore the application bravely.

"I saw him again the next day, and he assured me with genuine pleasure that every trace of the rheumatism had disappeared. I gave him some of my liniment, and also showed him some of the little pepper pods, so that he might procure them at any time in the future when he should need them.

"It was more than twenty years after this that I again met Joshua. He was then an elderly man, but still a vigorous soldier. He assured me that he had used my remedy whenever he had felt he least twinges of rheumatism, and that the disease had never interfered with the performance of his military duties.

"He was much surprised to see that I looked no older than

when he had met me before. He was greatly impressed by this, and talked a good deal about it. He told me he considered himself under the greatest obligations to me for what I had done for him, and as he spoke I could see that a hope was growing within him that perhaps I might do something more. He presently spoke out boldly, and said to me that as my knowledge of medicine had enabled me to keep myself from growing old, perhaps I could do the same thing for him. Few men had greater need of protecting themselves against the advance of old age. His work was not done, and years of bodily strength were necessary to enable him to finish it.

"But I could do nothing for Joshua in this respect. I assured him that my apparent exemption from the effects of passing years was perfectly natural, and was not due to drugs or medicaments.

"Joshua lived many years after that day, and did a good deal of excellent military work; but his life was not long enough to satisfy him. He fell sick, was obliged to give up his command to his relative Caleb, dying in his one hundred and twenty-eighth year."

"Which ought to satisfy him, I should say," said Mrs. Crowder.

"I have never yet met a thoroughbred worker," said Mr. Crowder, "who was satisfied to stop his work before he had finished it, no matter how old he might happen to be. But my last meeting with Joshua taught me a lesson which in those days had not been sufficiently impressed upon my mind. I became convinced that I must not allow people to think that I could live for twenty years or more without growing older, and after that I gave this matter a great deal more attention than I had yet bestowed upon it."

"It is a pity," said Mrs. Crowder, "that thy life should have been marred by such constant anxiety."

"Yes," said he; "but this is a suspicious world, and it is dangerous for a man to set himself apart from his fellow-beings, especially if he does it in some unusual fashion which people cannot understand."

"But I hope now," said his wife, "that those days of suspicion are entirely past." Now the conversation was getting awkward; it could not be pleasant for any one of us to talk about what the world of the future might think of Mr. Crowder when it came to know all about him, and, appreciating this, my host quickly changed the subject.

"There is a little story I have been wanting to tell you," said he, addressing his wife, "which I think would interest you. It is a love-story in which I was concerned."

"Oh!" said Mrs. Crowder, looking up quickly, "a scholar?"

"No," he answered; "not this time. Early in the fourteenth century I was living at Avignon, in the south of France. At that time I was making my living by copying law papers. You see, I was down in the world again."

Mrs. Crowder sighed, but said nothing.

"One Sunday morning I was in the Church of St. Claire, and, kneeling a little in front of me, I noticed a lady who did not seem to be paying the proper attention to her devotions. She fidgeted uneasily, and every now and then she would turn her head a little to the right, and then bring it back quickly and turn it so much in my direction that I could see the profile of her face. She was a good-looking woman, not very young, and evidently nervous and disturbed.

"Following the direction of her quick gaze when she again turned to the right, I saw a young man, apparently not twenty-five years of age, and dressed in sober black. He was also kneeling, but his eyes were steadfastly fixed upon the lady in front of me, and I knew, of course, that it was this continuous gaze which was disturbing her. I felt very much disposed to call the attention of a priest to this young man who was making one of the congregation unpleasantly conspicuous by staring at her; but the situation was brought to an end by the lady herself, who suddenly rose and went out of the church. She had no sooner passed the heavy leather curtain of the door than the young man got up and went out after her. Interested in this affair, I also left the church, and in the street I saw the lady walking rapidly away, with the young man at a respectful distance behind her.

"I followed on the other side of the street, determined to interfere if the youth, so evidently a stranger to the lady, should accost her or annoy her. She walked steadily on, not looking behind her, and doubtless hoping that she was not followed. As soon as she reached another church she turned and entered it. Without hesitation the young man went in after her, and then I followed.

"As before, the lady knelt on the pavement of the church, and the young man, placing himself not very far from her, immediately began to stare at her. I looked around, but there was no priest near, and then I advanced and knelt not very far from the lady, and between her and her persistent admirer. It was plain enough that he did not like this, and he moved forward so that he might still get a view of her. Then I also moved so as to obstruct his view. He now fixed his eyes upon me, and I returned his gaze in such a way as to make him understand that while I was present he would not be allowed to annoy a lady who evidently wished to have nothing to do with him. Presently he rose and went out. It was evident that he saw that it was no use for him to continue his reprehensible conduct while I was present. I do not know how the lady discovered that her unauthorized admirer had gone away, but she did discover it, and she turned toward me for an instant and gave me what I supposed was a look of gratitude.

PETRARCH AND LAURA.

"I soon left the church, and I had scarcely reached the street when I found that the lady had followed me. She looked at me as if she would like to speak, and I politely saluted her. 'I thank you, kind sir,' she said, 'for relieving me of the persistent attention of that young man. For more than a week he has followed me whenever I go to church, and although he has never spoken to me, his steady gaze throws me into such an agitation that I cannot think of my prayers. Do you know who he is, sir?'

"I assured her that I had never seen the youth before that morning, but that doubtless I could find out all about him. I told her that I was acquainted with several officers of the law, and that there would be no difficulty in preventing him from giving her any further annoyance. 'Oh, don't do that!' she said quickly. 'I would not wish to attract attention to myself in that way. You seem to be a kind and fatherly gentleman. Can you not speak to the young man himself and tell him who I am, and impress upon his mind how much he is troubling me by his inconsiderate action?'

"As I did not wish to keep her standing in the street, we now walked on together, and she briefly gave me the facts of the case.

"Her name was Mme. de Sade: she had been happily married for two years, and never before had she been annoyed by impertinent attentions from anyone; but in some manner unaccountable to her this young student had been attracted by her, and had made her the object of his attention whenever he had had the opportunity. Not only had he annoyed her at church, but twice he had followed her when she had left her house on business, thus showing that he had been loitering about in the vicinity. She had not yet spoken to her husband in the matter, because she was afraid that some quarrel might arise. But now that the good angels had caused her to meet with such a kind-hearted old gentleman as myself, she hoped that I might be able to rid her of the young man without making any trouble. Surely this student, who seemed to be a respectable person, would not think of such a thing as fighting me."

"Thee must have had a very long white beard at that time," interpolated Mrs. Crowder.

"Yes," he said; "I was in one of my periods of venerable age."

"I left Mme. de Sade, promising to do what I could for her, and as she thanked me I could not help wondering why the handsome young student had made her the object of his attention.

"She was a well-shaped, fairly good-looking woman, with light skin and large eyes; but she was of a grave and sober cast of countenance, and there was nothing about her which indicated the least of that piquancy which would be likely to attract the eyes of a youth. She seemed to me to be exactly what she said she was — the quiet and respectable lady of a quiet and respectable household.

"In the course of the afternoon I discovered the name and residence of the young man, with whom I had determined to have an interview. His name was Francesco Petrarca, an Italian by birth, and now engaged in pursuing his studies in this place. I called upon him at his lodgings, and, fortunately, found him at home. As I had expected, he recognized me at once as the elderly person who had interfered with him at the church; but, as I did not expect, he greeted me politely, without any resentment.

"I took the seat he offered me, and proceeded to deliver a lecture. I laid before him the facts of the case, which I supposed he might not know, and urged him, for his own sake, as well as for that of the lady, to cease his annoying and, I did not hesitate to state, ungentlemanly pursuit of her.

"He listened to me with respectful attention, and when I had finished he assured me that he knew even more about Mme. de

Sade than I did. He was perfectly aware that she was a religious and highly estimable lady, and he did not desire to do anything which would give her a moment's sorrow. 'Then stop following her,' said I, 'and give up that habit of staring at her in such a way as to make her the object of attention to everybody around her.' 'That is asking too much,' answered Master Petrarca. 'That lady has made an impression upon my soul which cannot be removed. My will would have no power to efface her image from my constant thought. If she does not wish me to do so, I shall never speak a word to her; but I must look upon her. Even when I sleep her face is present in my dreams. She has aroused within me the spirit of poetry; my soul will sing in praise of her loveliness, and I cannot prevent it. Let me read to you some lines,' he said, picking up a piece of manuscript which was lying on the table. 'It is in Italian, but I will translate it for you.' 'No,' said I; 'read it as it is written; I understand Italian.' Then he read the opening lines of a sonnet which was written to Laura in the shadow. He read about six lines and then stopped. 'It is not finished,' he said, 'and what I have written does not altogether satisfy me; but you can judge from what you have heard how it is that I think of that lady, and how impossible it is that I can in any way banish her from my mind, or willingly from my vision'

"'How did you come to know that her name is Laura?' I asked. 'I found it out from the records of her marriage,' he answered.

"I talked for some time to this young man, but failed to impress him with the conviction that his conduct was improper and unworthy of him. I found means to inform Mme. de Sade of the result of my conversation with Petrarch,—as we call his name in English,—and she appeared to be satisfied that the young student would soon cease his attentions, although I myself saw no reason for such belief.

"I visited the love-lorn young man several times, for I had become interested in him, and endeavored to make him see how foolish it was — even if he looked upon it in no other light — to direct his ardent affections upon a lady who would never care anything about him, and who, even if unmarried, was not the sort of woman who was adapted to satisfy the lofty affection which his words and his verses showed him to possess.

" 'There are so many beautiful women,' said I, 'any one of whom you might love, of whom you might sing, and to whom you could indite your verses. She would return your love, appreciate your poetry; you would marry her and be happy all your life.'

"He shook his head. 'No, no, no,' he said. 'You don't understand my nature. Marriage would mean the cares of a house — food, fuel, the mending of clothes, a family—all the hard material conditions of life. No, sir! My love soars far above all that. If it were possible that Laura should ever be mine I could not love her as I do. She is apart from me; she is above me. I worship her, and for her I pour out my soul in song. Listen to this,' and he read me some lines of an unfinished sonnet to Laura in the sunlight. 'She was just coming from a shaded street into an open place when I saw her, and this poem came into my heart.'

"About a week after this I was very much surprised to see Petrarch walking with his Laura, who was accompanied by her husband. The three were very amicably conversing. I joined the party, and was made acquainted with M. de Sade, and after that, from time to time, I met them together, sometimes taking a meal with them in the evening.

"I discovered that Laura's husband looked upon Petrarch very much as any ordinary husband would look upon an artist who wished to paint portraits of his wife.

"I lived for more than a year in Avignon with these good people, and I am not ashamed to say that I never ceased my endeavors to persuade Petrarch to give up his strange and abnormal attentions to a woman who would never be anything to him but a vision in the distance, and who would prevent him from living a true and natural life with one who would be all his own. But it was of no use; he went on in his own way, and everybody knows the results.

"Now, just think of it," continued Mr. Crowder. "Suppose I had succeeded in my honest efforts to do good; think of what the world would have lost. Suppose I had induced Petrarch not to come back to Avignon after his travels; suppose he had not settled down at Vaucluse, and had not spent three long years writing sonnets to Laura while she was occupied with the care of her large family of children; suppose, in a word, that I had been successful in my good work, and that Petrarch had shut his eyes and his heart to Laura; suppose—"

"I don't choose to suppose anything of the kind," said Mrs. Crowder. "Thee tried to do right, but I am glad thee did not deprive the world of any of Petrarch's poetry. But now I want thee to tell us something about ancient Egypt, and those wonderfully cultivated people who built pyramids and carved hieroglyphics. Perhaps thee saw them building the great Temple of the Sun at Heliopolis."

Mr. Crowder shook his head, saying, "That was before my time."

This was like an electric shock to both of us. If we had been more conversant with ancient chronology we might have understood, but we were not so conversant.

"Abraham! Isaac! Moses!" ejaculated Mrs. Crowder. "Thee knew them all, and yet Egypt was civilized before thy time! Does thee mean that?"

"Oh, yes," said Mr. Crowder. "I am of the time of Abraham, and when he was born the glories of Egypt were at their height."

"It is difficult to get these things straight in one's mind," said Mrs. Crowder. "As thee has lived so long, it seems a pity that thee was not born sooner."

"I have often thought that," said her husband; "but we should all try to be content with what we have. And now let us skip out of those regions of the dusky past. I feel in the humor of telling a love-story, and one has just come into my mind."

"Thee is so fond of that sort of thing," said his wife, with a smile, "that we will not interfere with thee."

"In the summer of the year 950," said Mr. Crowder, "I was traveling, and had just come over from France into the province of Piedmont, in northern Italy. I was then in fairly easy circumstances, and was engaged in making some botanical researches for a little book which I had planned to write on a medical subject. I will explain to you later how I came to do a great deal of that sort of thing.

"Late upon a warm afternoon I was entering the town of Ivrea, and passing a large stone building, I stopped to examine some leaves on a bush which grew by the roadside. While I was doing this, and comparing the shape and size of the leaves with some drawings I had in a book which I took from my pocket, I heard a voice behind me and apparently above me. Someone was speaking to me, and speaking in Latin. I looked around and up, but could see no one; but above me, about ten or twelve feet from the ground, there was a long, narrow slit of a window such as is seen in prisons. Again I heard the voice, and it said to me distinctly in Latin, 'Are you free to go where you choose?' It was the voice of a woman. As I wished to understand the situation better before I answered, I went over to the other side of the road, where I could get a better view of the window. There I saw behind this narrow opening a part of the face of a woman. This stone edifice was evidently a prison. I approached the window, and standing under it, first looking from side to side to see that no one was coming along the road, I said in Latin, 'I am free to go where I choose.'

"Then the voice above said, 'Wait!' but it spoke in Italian this time. You may be sure I waited, and in a few minutes a little package dropped from the window and fell almost at my feet. I stooped and picked it up. It was a piece of paper, in which was wrapped a bit of mortar to give it weight.

"I opened the paper and read, written in a clear and scholarly hand, these words: 'I am a most unfortunate prisoner. I believe you are an honest and true man, because I saw you studying plants and reading from a book which you carry. If you wish to do more good than you ever did before, come to this prison again after dark.'

"I looked up and said quickly, in Italian, 'I shall be here.' I was about to speak again and ask for some more definite directions, but I heard the sound of voices around a turn in the road, and I thought it better to continue my walk into the town.

"That night, as soon as it was really dark, I was again at the prison. I easily found the window, for I had noted that it was so many paces from a corner of the building; but there was no light in the narrow slit, and although I waited some time, I heard no voice. I did not dare to call, for the prisoner might not be alone, and I might do great mischief.

"My eyes were accustomed to the darkness, and it was starlight. I walked along the side of the building, examining it carefully, and I soon found a little door in the wall. As I stood for a few moments before this door, it suddenly opened, and in front of me stood a big soldier. He wore a wide hat and a little sword, and evidently was not surprised to see me. I thought it well, however, to speak, and I said: 'Could you give a mouthful of supper to a—'

"He did not allow me to finish my sentence, but putting his hand upon my shoulder, said gruffly: 'Come in. Don't you waste your breath talking about supper.' I entered, and the door was closed behind me. I followed this man through a stone passage-way, and he took me to a little stone room. 'Wait here!' he said, and he shut me in. I was in pitch-darkness, and had no idea what was going to happen next. After a little time I saw a streak of light coming through a keyhole; then an inner door opened, and a young woman with a lamp came into the room."

"Now does the love-story begin?" asked his wife.

"Not yet," said Mr. Crowder. "The, young woman looked at me, and I looked at her. She was a pretty girl with black eyes. I did not express my opinion of her, but she was not so reticent. 'You look like a good old man,' she said. 'I think you may be trusted. Come!' Her speech was provincial, and she was plainly a servant. I followed her. 'Now for the mistress,' said I to myself."

"Thee may have looked like an old man," remarked Mrs. Crowder, "but thee did not think like one."

Her husband laughed. "I mounted some stone steps, and was soon shown into a room where stood a lady waiting for me. As the light of the lamp carried by the maid fell upon her face, I thought I had never seen a more beautiful woman. Her dress, her carriage, and her speech showed her to be a lady of rank. She was very young, scarcely twenty, I thought.

"This lady immediately began to ask me questions. She had perceived that I was a stranger, and she wanted to know where I came from, what was my business, and as much as I could tell her of myself. 'I knew you were a scholar,' she said, 'because of your book, and I believe in scholars.' Then briefly she told me her story and what she wanted of me.

"She was the young Queen Adelheid, the widow of King Lothar, who had recently died, and she was then suffering a series of harsh persecutions from the present king, Berengar II, who in this way was endeavoring to force her to marry his son Adalbert. She hated this young man, and positively refused to have anything to do with him.

"This charming and royal young widow was bright, intelligent, and had a mind of her own; it was easy to see that. She had formed a scheme for her deliverance, and she had been waiting to find someone to help her carry it out. Now, she thought I was the man she had been looking for. I was elderly, apparently respectable, and she had to trust somebody.

"This was her scheme. She was well aware that unless some powerful friend interfered on her behalf she would be obliged to marry Adalbert, or remain in prison for the rest of her life, which would probably be unduly shortened. Therefore, she had made up her mind to appeal to the court of the Emperor Otto I of Germany, and she wanted me to carry a letter to him.

"I stood silent, earnestly considering this proposition, and as I did so she gazed at me as if her whole happiness in this world depended upon my decision. I was not long in making up my mind on the subject. I told her that I was willing to help her, and would undertake to carry a letter to the emperor, and I did not doubt, from what I had heard of this noble prince, that he would come to her deliverance. But I furthermore assured her that the moment it became known that the emperor was about to interfere on her behalf, she would be in a position of great danger, and would probably disappear from human sight before relief could reach her. In that prison she was utterly helpless, and to appeal for help would be to bring down vengeance upon herself. The first thing to do, therefore, was to escape from this prison, and get to some place where, for a time at least, she could defend herself against Berengar, while waiting for Otto to take her under his protection.

"She saw the force of my remarks, and we discussed the matter for half an hour, and when I left—being warned by the soldier on guard, who was in love with the queen's black-eyed maid, that it was time for me to depart—it was arranged that I should return the next night and confer with the fair Adelheid.

"There were several conferences, and the unfaithful sentinel grumbled a good deal. I cannot speak of all the plans and projects which we discussed, but at last one of them was carried out. One dark, rainy night Adelheid changed clothes with her maid, actually deceived the guard—not the fellow who had admitted me—with a story that she had been sent in great haste to get some medicine for her royal mistress, and joined me outside the prison.

"There we mounted horses I had in readiness, and rode away from Ivrea. We were bound for the castle of Canossa, a stronghold of considerable importance, where my royal companion believed she could find refuge, at least for a time. I cannot tell you of all the adventures we had upon that difficult journey. We were pursued; we were almost captured; we met with obstacles of various kinds, which sometimes seemed insurmountable; but at last we saw the walls of Canossa rising before us, and we were safe.

"Adelheid was very grateful for what I had done, and as she had now learned to place full reliance upon me, she insisted that I should be the bearer of a letter from her to the Emperor Otto. I should not travel alone, but be accompanied by a sufficient retinue of soldiers and attendants, and should go as her ambassador.

"The journey was a long and a slow one, but I was rather glad of it, for it gave me an opportunity to ponder over the most ambitious scheme I have ever formed in the whole course of my life."

"Greater than to be autocrat of all the Russias?" exclaimed Mrs. Crowder. "Yes," he replied. "That opportunity came to me suddenly, and I accepted it; I did not plan it out and work for it. Besides, it could be only a transitory thing. But what now occupied me was a grand idea, the good effects of which, if it should be carried out, might endure for centuries. It was simply this:

"I had become greatly attached to the young queen widow whose cause I had espoused. I had spent more than a month with her in the castle at Canossa, and there I learned to know her well and to love her. She was, indeed, a most admirable woman and charming in every way. She appeared to place the most implicit trust in me; told me of all her affairs, and asked my opinion about almost everything she proposed to do. In a word, I was in love with her and wanted to marry her."

"Thee certainly had lofty notions; but don't think I object," said Mrs. Crowder. "It is the Chinese and Tartars that I don't like."

"It might seem at first sight," he continued, "that I was aiming above me, but the more I reflected the more firmly I believed that it would be very good for the lady, as well as for me. In the first place, she had no reason to expect a matrimonial union worthy of her. Adalbert she had every reason to despise, and there was no one else belonging to the riotous aristocratic factions of Italy who could make her happy or give her a suitable position. In all her native land there was not a prince to whom she would not have to stoop in order to marry him.

"But to me she need not stoop. No man on earth possessed a more noble lineage. I was of the house of Shem, a royal priest after the order of Melchizedek, and King of Salem! No line of imperial ancestry could claim precedence of that."

Mrs. Crowder looked with almost reverent awe into the face of her husband. "And that is the blood," she said, "which flows in the veins of our child?"

"Yes," said he, "that is the blood." After a slight pause Mr. Crowder continued: "I will now go on with my tale of ambition. A grand career would open before me. I would lay all my plans and hopes before the Emperor Otto, who would naturally be inclined to assist the unfortunate widow; but he would be still more willing to do so when I told him of the future which might await her if my plans should be carried out. As he was then engaged in working with a noble ambition for the benefit of his own dominions, he would doubtless be willing to do something for the good of lands beyond his boundaries. It ought not to be difficult to convince him that there could be no wiser, no nobler way of championing the cause of Adelheid than by enabling me to perform the work I had planned.

"All that would be necessary for him to do would be to furnish me with a moderate military force. With this I would march to Canossa; there I would espouse Adelheid; then I would proceed to Ivrea, would dethrone the wicked Berengar, would proclaim Adelheid queen in his place, with myself as king consort; then, with the assistance and backing of the imperial German, I would no doubt soon be able to maintain my royal pretensions. Once self-supporting, and relying upon our Italian subjects for our army and finances, I would boldly reestablish the great kingdom of Lombardy, to which Charlemagne had put an end nearly two hundred years before. Then would begin a grand system of reforms and national progress.

"Pavia should be my capital, but the beneficent influence of my rule should move southward. I would make an alliance with the Pope; I would crush and destroy the factions which were shaking the foundations of church and state; I would still further extend my power — I would become the imperial ruler of Italy, with Adelheid as my queen!

"Over and over again I worked out and arranged this grand scheme, and when I reached the court of the Emperor Otto it was all as plain in my mind as if it had been copied on parchment.

"I was very well received by the emperor, and he read with great interest and concern the letter I had brought him. He gave me several private audiences, and asked me many questions about the fair young widow who had met with so many persecutions and misfortunes. This interest greatly pleased me, but I did not immediately submit to him my plan for the relief of Adelheid and the great good of the Italian nation. I would wait a little; I must make him better acquainted with myself. But the imperial Otto did not wait. On the third day after my arrival I was called into his cabinet and informed that he intended to set out himself at the head of an army; that he should relieve the unfortunate lady from her persecutions and establish her in her rights, whatever they might prove to be. His enthusiastic manner in speaking of his intentions assured me that I need not trouble myself to say one word about my plans.

"Now, — would you believe it? — that intermeddling monarch took out of my hands the whole grand, ambitious scheme I had so carefully devised. He went to Canossa; he married Adelheid; he marched upon Berengar; he subjugated him and made him his vassal; he formed an alliance with Pope John XII; he was proclaimed King of the Lombards; he was crowned with his queen in St. Peter's; he eventually acquired the southern portion of Italy. All this was exactly what I had intended to do."

Mrs. Crowder laughed. "In one way thee was served quite right, for thee made all thy plans without ever asking the beautiful young, ex-queen whether she would have thee or not." In the tones of this fair lady's voice there were evident indications of mental relief. "And what did thee do then?" she asked. "I hope thee got some reward for all thy faithful exertions."

"I received nothing at the time," Mr. Crowder replied; "and as I did not care to accompany the emperor into Italy, for probably I would be recognized as the man who had assisted Adelheid to escape from the prison at Ivrea, and as I was not at all sure that the emperor would remember that I needed protection, I thought it well to protect myself, and so I journeyed back into France as well as I could.

"This was not very well; for in purchasing the necessary fine clothes which I deemed it proper to wear in the presence of the royal lady whose interests I had in charge, in buying horses, and in many incidental expenses, I had spent my money. I was too proud to ask Otto to reimburse me, for that would have been nothing but charity on his part; and of course I could not expect the fair Adelheid to think of my possible financial needs. So, away I went, a poor wanderer on foot, and the imperial Otto rode forward to love, honor, and success."

"A dreadful shame!" exclaimed Mrs. Crowder. "It seems as if thee always carried a horn about with thee so that thee might creep out of the little end of it."

"But my adventures with Adelheid did not end here," he said. "About fifty years after this she was queen regent in Italy, during the infancy of her grandchild Otto III. Being in Rome, and very poor, I determined to go to her, not to seek for charity, but to recall myself to her notice, and to boldly ask to be reimbursed for my expenses when assisting her to escape from Ivrea, and in afterward going as her ambassador to Otto I. In other words, I wanted to present my bill for enabling her to take her seat upon the throne of the 'Holy Roman Empire of the German Nation.'

"As a proof that I was the man I assumed to be, I took with me a ring of no great value, but set with her royal seal, which she had given me when she sent me to Otto.

"Well, I will not spend much time on this part of the story. By means of the ring I was accorded an interview with the regent. She was then an old woman over seventy years of age. When I introduced myself to her and told her my errand, she became very angry. 'I remember very well,' she said, 'the person you speak of, and he is long since dead. He was an old man when I took him into my service. You may be his son or someone else who has heard how he was employed by me. At any rate, you are an impostor. How did you come into possession of this ring? The man to whom I gave it had no right to keep it. He should have returned it to me when he had performed his duties.'

"I tried to convince her that there was no reason to suppose that the man who had assisted her could not be living at this day. He need only be about one hundred years old, and that age was not uncommon. I affirmed most earnestly that the ring had never been out of my possession, and that I should not have come to her if I had not believed that she would remember my services, and be at least willing to make good the considerable sums I had expended in her behalf.

"Now she arose in royal wrath. 'How dare you speak to me in that way!' she said. 'You are a younger man at this moment than that old stranger you represent yourself to be.' Then she called her guards and had me sent to prison as a cheat and an impostor. I remained in prison for some time, but as no definite charge was made against me, I was not brought to trial, and after a time was released to make room for somebody else. I got away as soon as I could, and thus ended my most ambitious dream."

CHAPTER SEVEN

"NOW, MY DEAR," said Mr. Crowder, regarding his wife with a tender kindness which I had frequently noticed in him, "just for a change, I know you would like to hear of a career of prosperity, wouldn't you?"

"Indeed, I would!" said Mrs. Crowder.

"You will have noticed," said her husband, "that there has been a great deal of variety in my vocations; in fact, I have not mentioned a quarter of the different trades and callings in which I have been engaged. It was sometimes desirable and often absolutely necessary for me to change my method of making a living, but during one epoch of my life I steadily devoted myself to a single profession.

"For nearly four hundred years I was engaged almost continuously in the practice of medicine. I found it easier for me, as a doctor, to change my place of residence and to appear in a new country with as much property as I could carry about with me, than if I had done so in any other way. A prosperous and elderly man coming as a stranger from a far country would, under ordinary circumstances, be regarded with suspicion unless he were able to give some account of his previous career. But a doctor from a far country was always welcome; if he could cure people of their ailments they did not ask anything about the former circumstances of his life. It was perfectly natural for a learned man to travel."

"Did thee regularly study and go to college?" asked Mrs. Crowder, "or was thee a quack?"

"Oh, I studied," said her husband, smiling, "and under the best masters. I had always a fancy for that sort of thing, and in the days of the patriarchs, when there were no regular doctors, I was often called upon, as I told you."

"Oh, yes," said his wife; "thee rubbed Joshua with gravel and pepper."

"And cured him," said he. "You ought not to have omitted that. But it was not until about the fifth century before Christ that I thought of really studying medicine. I was in the island of Cos, where I had gone for a very queer reason. The great painter Apelles lived there, and I went for the purpose of studying art under him. I was tired of most of the things I had been doing, and I thought it would be a good idea to become a painter. Apelles gave me no encouragement when I applied to him; he told me I was entirely too old to become a pupil. 'By the time you would really know how to paint,' said he, 'supposing you have any talent for it, you ought to be beginning to arrange your affairs to get ready to die.' Of course, this admonition had no effect upon me, and I kept on with my drawing lessons. If I could not become a painter of eminence, I thought that at least I might be able, if I understood drawing, to become a better schoolmaster — if I should take up that profession again.

"One day Apelles said to me, after glancing at the drawing on which I was engaged: 'If you were ten years younger you might do something in the field of art, for you would make an excellent model for the picture I am about to begin. But at your present age you would not be able to sustain the fatigue of remaining in a constrained position for any length of time.' 'What is the subject?' I asked. 'A centurion in battle,' said he.

"The next day I appeared before Apelles with my hair cropped short and my face without a vestige of a beard. 'Do I look young enough now to be your model?' said I. The painter looked at me in surprise. 'Yes,' said he, 'you look young enough; but of course you are the same age as you were yesterday. However, if you would like to try the model business, I will make some sketches of you.'

"For more than a month, nearly every day, I stood as a model to Apelles for his great picture of a centurion whose sword had been stricken from his hand, and who, in desperation, was preparing to defend himself against his enemy with the arms which nature had given him."

"Is that picture extant?" I asked.

Mr. Crowder smiled. "None of Apelles's paintings are in existence now," he answered. "While I was acting as model to Apelles — and I may remark that I never grew tired of standing in the position he desired—I listened with great satisfaction to the conversations between him and the friends who called upon him while he was at work. The chief of these was Hippocrates, the celebrated physician, between whom and Apelles a strong friendship existed.

"Hippocrates was a man of great common sense. He did not believe that diseases were caused by spirits and demons and all that sort of thing, and in many ways he made himself very interesting to me. So, in course of time, after having visited him a good deal, I made up my mind to quit the study of art and go into that of medicine.

"I got on very well, and after a time I practised with him in many cases, and he must have had a good deal of confidence in me, for when the King of Persia sent for him to come to his court, offering him all sorts of munificent rewards, Hippocrates declined, but he suggested to me that I should go.

" 'You look like a doctor,' said he. 'The king would have confidence in you simply on account of your presence; and, besides, you do know a great deal about medicine. But I did not go to Persia, and shortly after that I left the island of Cos and gave up the practice of medicine. Later, in the second century before Christ, I made the acquaintance of a methodist doctor—"

"A what? "Mrs. Crowder and I exclaimed at the same moment.

He laughed. "I thought that would surprise you, but it is true."

"Of course it is true," said his wife, coloring a little. "Does thee think I would doubt anything thee told me? If thee had said that Abraham had a Quaker cook, I would have believed it."

"And if I had told you that," said Mr. Crowder, "it would have been so. But to explain about this methodist doctor. In those days the physicians were divided into three schools: empirics, dogmatists, and methodists. This man I speak of—Asclepiades—was the leading methodist physician, depending, as the name suggests, upon regular methods of treatment instead of experiments and theories adapted to the particular case in hand.

"He also was a man of great good sense, and was very witty besides. He made a good deal of fun of other physicians, and used to call the system of Hippocrates 'meditation on death.' I studied with him for some time, but it was not until the first century of the present era that I really began the practice of my profession. Then I made the acquaintance of the great Galen. He was a man who was not only a physician, but an accomplished surgeon, and this could be said of very few people in that age of the world. I studied anatomy and surgery under him, and afterward practised with him as I had done with Hippocrates.

"The study of anatomy was rather difficult in those days, because the Roman laws forbade the dissection of citizens, and the anatomists had to depend for their knowledge of the human frame upon their examinations of the bodies of enemies killed in battle, or those of slaves, in whom no one took an interest; but most of all upon the bodies of apes. Great numbers of these beasts were brought from Africa solely for the use of the Roman surgeons, and in that connection I remember an incident which was rather curious.

"I had not finished my studies under Galen when that great master one day informed me that a trader had brought him an ape, which had been confined in a small building near his house. He asked me to go out and kill it and have it brought into his dissecting-room, where he was about to deliver a lecture to some students.

"I started for the building referred to. On the way I was met by the trader. He was a vile-looking man, with black, matted hair and little eyes, who did not look much higher in intelligence than the brutes he dealt in. He grinned diabolically as he led me to the little house and opened the door. I looked in. There was no ape there, but in one corner sat a dark-brown African girl. I looked at the man in surprise. 'The ape I was to bring got away from me,' he said, 'but that thing will do a great deal better, and I will not charge any more for it than for the ape. Kill it, and we will put it into a bag and carry it to the doctor. He will be glad to see what we have brought him instead of an ape.'

"I angrily ordered the man to leave the place, and taking the girl by the arm, although I had a good deal of trouble in catching her,—I led her to Galen and told him the story."

"And what became of the poor thing?" asked Mrs. Crowder.

"Galen bought her from the man at the price of an ape, and

tried to have her educated as a servant, but she was a wild creature and could not be taught much. In some way or other the people in charge of the amphitheater got possession of her, and I heard that she was to figure in the games at an approaching great occasion. I was shocked and grieved to hear this, for I had taken an interest in the girl, and I knew what it meant for her to take part in the games in the arena. I tried to buy her, but it was of no use: she was wanted for a particular purpose. On the day she was to appear in the arena I was there."

"I don't see how thee could do it," said Mrs. Crowder, her face quite pale.

"People's sensibilities were different in those days," said her husband. "I don't suppose I could do such a thing now. After a time she was brought out and left entirely alone in the middle of the great space. She was nearly frightened to death by the people and the fear of some unknown terror. Trembling from head to foot, she looked from side to side, and at last sank crouching on the ground. Everybody was quiet, for it was not known what was to happen next. Then a grating sound was heard, with the clank of an iron door, and a large brown bear appeared in the arena. The crouching African fixed her eyes upon him, but did not move.

"The idea of a combat between this tender girl and a savage bear could not be entertained. What was about to occur seemed simply a piece of brutal carnage, with nothing to make it interesting. A great many people expressed their dissatisfaction. The hardhearted populace, even if they did not care about fair play in their games, did desire some element of chance which would give flavor to the cruelty. But here was nothing of the sort. It would have been as well to feed the beast with a sheep.

"The bear, however, seemed to look upon the performance as one which would prove very satisfactory. He was hungry, not having had anything to eat for several days, and here was an appetizing young person waiting for him to devour her.

"He had fixed his eyes upon her the moment he appeared, and had paid no attention whatever to the crowds by which he was, surrounded. He gave a slight growl, the hair on his neck stood up, and he made a quick movement toward the girl. But she did not wait for him. Springing to her feet, she fled, the bear after her.

"Now followed one of the most exciting chases ever known in the history of the Roman amphitheater. That frightened girl, as swift as a deer, ran around and around the vast space, followed closely by her savage pursuer. But although he was active and powerful and unusually swift for a bear, he could not catch her.

"Around and around she went, and around went the red-eyed beast behind her; but he could not gain upon her, and she gave no sign that her strength was giving out.

"Now the audience began to perceive that a contest was really going on: it was a contest of speed and endurance, and the longer the girl ran the more inclined the people were to take her part. At last there was a great shout that she should be allowed to escape. A little door was opened in the side of the amphitheater; she shot through it, and it was closed almost in the face of the panting and furious bear."

"What became of the poor girl?" exclaimed Mrs. Crowder.

"A sculptor bought her," said Mr. Crowder. "He wanted to use her as a model for a statue of the swift Diana; but this never came to anything. The girl could not be made to stand still for a moment. She was in a chronic condition of being frightened to death. After that I heard of her no more; it was easy for people to disappear in Rome. But this incident in the arena was remembered and talked about for many years afterward. The fact that a girl was possessed of such extraordinary swiftness that she would have

"'THE CROUCHING AFRICAN FIXED HER EYES UPON HIM.'"

been able to escape from a wild beast, by means of her speed alone, had she been in an open plain, was considered one of the most interesting natural wonders which had been brought to the notice of the Roman people by the sports in the arena."

"Fortunately," said Mrs. Crowder, "thee did not—"

"No," said her husband, "I did not. I required more than speed in a case like that. And now I think," said he, rising, "we must call this session concluded."

The next day I was obliged to bid farewell to the Crowders, and my business arrangements made it improbable that I should see them again for a long time—I could not say how long. As I bade Mr. Crowder farewell and stood holding his hand in mine, he smiled, and said: "That's right. Look hard at me; study every line in my face, and then when you see me again you will be better able—"

"Not a bit," said Mrs. Crowder. "He is just as able to judge now as he will be if he stays away for twenty years."

I believed her, as I warmly shook her hand, and I believe that I shall always continue to believe her.

THE END

www.ingramcontent.com/pod-product-compliance
Lightning Source LLC
Chambersburg PA
CBHW030427310726
48979CB00009B/1650/J
9781932490077